FINDING
You

the SEX ON THE BEACH series

FINDING
You

the SEX ON THE BEACH series

NEW YORK TIMES AND USA TODAY BESTSELLING AUTHOR
JENNA BENNETT

Photograph:
Cover Design: Sarah Hansen, OkayCreations.com
Interior Design: E.M. Tippetts Book Designs
emtippettsbookdesigns.com

ISBN: 978-0-9899434-9-9

Magpie Ink

For Jen and Jennifer, to much success and nothing but good times ahead.

Prologue

My relationship with Ty Connor lasted six months before hitting the skids.

We met in Key West in March, he came to Chicago in May, and we broke up the day before Thanksgiving.

It wasn't because of another girl, or even another guy. It wasn't because I didn't love him anymore. It wasn't because he didn't love me. He said he did, and I believed him.

No, it was a lot simpler than that.

It was his job.

I was still in college, finishing up my last year at UC. Journalism. Ty was four years older, and had been working for the FBI for the past two years.

Yes, *that* FBI. My boyfriend was a Fed. An undercover agent. That's how I met him. He'd been in Florida for Spring Break to catch a serial rapist, one who preyed on college girls coming to Key West to get drunk and get laid. I got involved in the investigation when I got involved with Ty, and things escalated from there.

The bad guy was behind bars now, and would go on trial in March, just as Spring Break was about to kick off again. I'd have to fly down to testify.

But after all that went down, Ty transferred to the Chicago office so we could be together. And my life was complete—sort of—until I learned that life with an FBI agent is hard.

We'd been dating for less than a month the first time he disappeared.

All I got was a text on my way to class one morning:

Gotta go to work. Back in a week. Love U.

Sure.

I mean, I worried, of course. I knew what he did for a living. He hunted down rapists and infiltrated street gangs and arrested drug dealers and had the occasional run-in with pedophiles who had convinced him to cross state lines for immoral purposes, violating something he said was called the Mann Act. He dealt with a lot of bad people. Bad things could happen to him. Someone could hurt him, or kill him. He could disappear—really disappear—and I'd never know what happened.

A week passed, and he didn't write and he didn't call. I got angry, and then I got scared, and then I got more angry and more scared. I also didn't sleep, and missed a couple of assignments I should have aced because I was too tired to think straight. If this kept up, I'd end up having to take my last year of college again, and that wouldn't make my parents happy. Me either, for that matter.

He returned a couple of weeks later, like nothing was wrong, and after I'd hugged him and kissed him and touched him and made sure he was in one piece, he told me that this was the way it was going to be. The Bureau needed him to go undercover, so he went. He was good at it. He could still pass for seventeen with a little effort. There weren't a lot of agents who could, so it was important that he do what he could while he could still do it. If I didn't want to deal with that, he'd be sorry, but he'd understand.

How do you tell a hero—someone who puts his own life on the line to make sure you and other people are safe—that your worry about his safety and your GPA are more important than what he's doing?

You don't. So I sucked it up. Because I loved him, and wanted to be with him. When he was around, it was great. It was the times he wasn't around that were the problem.

But I stuck it out. Until Thanksgiving, when I couldn't handle it anymore.

We were headed to my hometown in Ohio to spend the holiday with my mom and dad, and the day before we were set to leave, Ty came and told me he couldn't go.

I guess I should be grateful that he told me. He could have just left again, with a text when it was too late to do anything about it. So it was actually very nice of him to give me advance notice. But it just became too much.

"It's Thanksgiving!"

"Gangs don't stop dealing drugs because it's a holiday," Ty said.

"Isn't there someone else who can go? We had plans!"

"Cassie." He put his arms around me. "We've talked about this."

I fisted my hands against his chest. Part of me wanted to pummel him, and part of me wanted to grab fistfuls of his shirt and hang on. I didn't do either. "My mom and dad were looking forward to meeting you."

"I know. I'm sorry." He nuzzled my cheek and my ear, his breath warm. "It's the job."

The nuzzling was nice, but not nice enough. "I don't think I can do this, Ty," I told his shoulder. "I love you. I want us to be together. But I don't think I can do this anymore. Every time you disappear, I worry that you won't come back. And then you do, and I worry that you'll leave again." And so on, in a vicious cycle that I knew had no end. Until the one time he didn't come back, would never come back—and since I didn't even want to think about that possibility, I forced my mind back to the present.

If this had been a stupid romance novel, he would have told me he'd always come back. Like he was some kind of super-hero.

He didn't. Instead, he was honest. "I try to be careful. You know that."

I swallowed. "I know. It just isn't enough."

When he dropped his hands from my waist, I wanted to cry, to change my mind, to tell him to hold on and not let go.

I didn't. I dropped my own hands from his chest instead, and took a step back. "I'm sorry."

His eyes were the bright green of emeralds. "Me, too."

"It isn't that I don't love you."

He nodded. "I know."

"Take care of yourself. Please."

My eyes were swimming with tears. When he leaned in to drop a soft kiss on my cheek, I couldn't see him clearly.

"You, too," he told me. And then he stepped back. I didn't blink until he was through the door and out of sight, because I didn't want to watch him walk away. The tears kept my eyes nicely blurry, and that's the way I wanted it. It wasn't until I heard the door slam on the first floor, that I knew he was really gone.

CHAPTER

The Florida Keys looked just the same a year later. Lots of turquoise water, white sand, and almost-naked people. The difference…

Well, there were a lot of differences. I was coming in alone, for one thing. Last year, my best friends Mackenzie and Quinn and I had come down together. And since Mackenzie had been footing the bill, we'd been staying at a gorgeous high-rise hotel right in the middle of Party Central.

This year, I was alone, and paying my own way. And since Mackenzie is a successful country music singer, while I'm a struggling college student, I could kiss the high-rise goodbye. The airport shuttle dropped me outside Richardson's Motel. Nowhere near the middle of Party Central; down toward the southern shore of Key West, but close enough that I could walk to Duval Street.

Ty had been staying here last year, so I figured it was safe. The FBI wouldn't put one of their agents up in a place that wasn't. And because it was out of the way and a little past its prime, the price was right, too.

The same guy as a year ago was perched on a stool behind the counter in the office. I think he was wearing the same T-shirt: green, with a Wizards of the Coast logo. And he might be reading the same magazine: something Japanese, with tentacles.

When I walked in, wheeling my suitcase behind me, he looked up. And blinked, but didn't say anything to indicate that he remembered me from last year. Just waited for me to speak first. "Cassandra Wilder," I told him. "I've booked a room for the next two weeks."

Spring Break was actually a week from now. And Quinn and Mackenzie were both coming. Quinn would be bringing her boyfriend James, the struggling artist AKA Ivy League Dude, who was even wealthier than Mackenzie. Or at least he had been, until he gave up all the money to prove to Quinn—and I guess to himself—that he could make it on his own.

Mackenzie was finishing up a concert tour, and would be landing in Key West toward the end of next week. Her boyfriend Austin was supposed to be coming as well, but last I heard something had gone wrong there, and she'd been talking about breaking up with him. Something about a girl in his dressing room, and an article in some magazine. We'd all gotten used to the lies the paparazzi told, but this one wasn't a lie, or at least Mac thought it wasn't. I was a little confused about the whole thing, but that could be because I had other things on my mind.

The trial of Stan Laszlo, the rapist from last year, had started today. I guess it was someone's bright idea to time it to coincide with Spring Break a year later, to show how seriously Key West law enforcement took the safety of the tourists. There was very little doubt Stan would get hit with a whopping sentence, and that would make the police look good and all the Spring Breakers feel safe. They'd drink and party and spend more money, and everyone would be happy.

Except those of us involved with the trial, I guess. It wasn't so bad for me, but I'm sure the girls he had drugged and assaulted weren't looking forward to talking about it.

Stan had attacked me, but since the police had been watching, he'd been pulled off and arrested before he could do any real damage. I'd volunteered to be bait, after it became obvious to all of us that I'd become a target. Stan had seen me with Ty, and he knew Ty was there to catch him, so going after me must have seemed like a good idea. If he could get away with it, it would destroy Ty, on both a professional and a personal level.

I don't think it occurred to him—Stan—that he wouldn't get away with it. He'd always gotten away with it before, so he probably thought he was invincible.

Surprise.

And now he was on trial, and I had to testify. Which was why I was here, looking at the specimen with the scraggly beard and shifty eyes.

Wizard Dude didn't give any indication he remembered me. Nor did he seem curious as to why I was there a week earlier than all the other Spring Breakers. He didn't speak at all, just shoved a piece of paper and a pen in my direction and pointed at the line where he wanted me to sign. When I had, he put a key on the counter. A real key, not one of those high-end keycards the high-rise hotels have. This was your basic Yale on a ring with a turquoise plastic tag. The number 102 was written on it in black magic marker.

"Thank you," I said.

He nodded. By the time I walked out the door, he was already deep into the tentacle porn again.

Richardson's Motel consisted of an A-shaped building where the office was, and in each direction, a wing of rooms. The whole thing was painted white with a cheerful red roof and bright turquoise doors. Outside each door sat a planter with red flowers. And while I'd been here once before, looking for Ty, he hadn't been in, so I hadn't seen any of the rooms. It was with a bit of trepidation I inserted the key into the lock of room 102 and pushed the door open.

It could have been worse, and that's about the best I can say for it.

It was clean, mostly, but quite worn. The furnishings were 1970s motel style: a basic bed with a low headboard, a dresser with three drawers, a table and chair over by the window. A small microwave on top of an apartment-size fridge in lieu of a bedside table. The bathroom had a sink, a shower, and a toilet, all functional but not at all pretty. The only nice thing about the place was the bouquet of flowers sitting on the table. Lilies and carnations and some sort of little spriggy things, with a small card perched against the vase.

My heart skipped a beat.

I hadn't seen Ty since he'd walked out my door the day before Thanksgiving. I had no idea whether he was still in Chicago, or whether he'd transferred to another FBI field office after we broke up. For all I knew, he could be working out of San Francisco or Miami by now. He hadn't tried to contact me, and I appreciated it, since seeing him again would only make things worse.

I missed him terribly. I knew he'd be in Key West this week—he had to testify, too—and I couldn't wait to lay eyes on him. The fact that it had been more than three months since the last time I saw him, hadn't made any difference at all. The possibility that the flowers might be from him sent my heart into a fluttering of anticipation.

Except they weren't. The card was from the Key West PD, or more specifically from one Detective Enrique—Ricky— Fuentes. He was the guy who'd been standing by to yank Stan off me and slap handcuffs on him last March. The Key West detective in charge of the case.

I turned the card over to check the back, but he hadn't left any kind of message. I guess maybe he didn't want it to look like he was communicating with me in secret. The cop in charge of the case talking privately to one of the key witnesses was something the defense could use to cause a lot of trouble.

I didn't want it to look like I was conspiring with him, either—and I figured I'd probably see him in court and could find a moment to thank him for the flowers then—so I didn't use the phone number or email address on the card to contact him.

Instead, I emptied my suitcase into the bureau drawers and my toiletries onto the vanity in the bathroom before I gave my hair a swipe with a brush and headed out. I'd caught a morning flight out of Chicago, so it was still just early afternoon here. I needed something to eat, and I wanted to stop by the courthouse before my own testimony tomorrow, so I'd have some idea what it would look and feel like. It never hurts to be prepared.

The food was easy: I grabbed a hot dog from I Dream of Weenie and munched while I walked. The Courthouse was a bit of a trek, but the weather was nice—especially considering how cold it still was in Chicago—and there's always plenty to look at in Key West.

The Courthouse was located in the Old Town, just on the corner of Thomas and Fleming. It was a Victorian building: two-story red brick with tall, white pillars, arched windows, and a square clock tower. The words Monroe County Court House and the year 1890 were written on the front, above the second floor balcony.

I pushed through the double front doors—louvered, to allow for the breeze to come in; no A/C in 1890—and a set of much more modern metal detectors, to find myself in a wide hallway with doors on either side. A security guard had been standing by the wall, and now he came toward me.

"Afternoon, miss." He held out a hand the size of a ham. "Purse, please."

I lifted the strap over my head and gave it to him.

He gave me a look from under bushy brows. "Name and business?"

"Cassandra Wilder," I said, watching as he unzipped my shoulder bag and stuck his hand in. "I'm testifying against Stan Laszlo tomorrow. I wanted to see what to expect."

He didn't respond to that, just pulled an emery board out of my bag. One of the bushy eyebrows lifted.

"Nail file," I said.

He put the tip of a finger against the point and tested it. And must have decided I couldn't do much damage with such a wimpy implement, because he dropped it back into the purse again. "Last door on the right."

"Thank you." I looped the bag back over my head and headed that way.

A piece of paper in a frame to the right of the door said State vs. Laszlo. I pushed the handle down slowly, careful not to make any noise, and pushed the door in. It didn't squeak. The voice from inside became audible as more than just a murmur. "—been acquainted with the defendant?"

The woman on the witness stand was a couple of years older than me, and a knockout. Long, black hair, big, brown eyes, puffy lips, and eyelashes for days. Not to mention the figure—although I won't. The first time I saw Carmen Fuentes, she was wearing a tank top that said *Save a Virgin – Do Me Instead*, and she was flirting with Ty. I'd hated her on sight. It wasn't until later that I found out she was Detective Fuentes's sister, and Ty's liaison with the police department, because nobody would think anything of it if he couldn't stay away from her. We even made friends, sort of, later on.

There was no *Save a Virgin* tank on display today. Carmen was dressed in a crisp white shirt, one with three-quarter length sleeves and no hint of cleavage. Someone must have told her to dress down for the occasion.

Not that it made a difference. She was still a knockout, even with her hair scraped back from her face into a bun, and nude lipstick. Even her voice was more subdued than I remember it as she answered the question. "We both grew up in Key West. We went to school together. I've known Stan most of my life."

"And were you ever involved?"

"No," Carmen said.

"You never dated?"

She shook her head.

"Out loud for the record, please."

"No," Carmen said. "We never went out. Never dated. Never were involved. He asked me out, but I always said no."

I slipped onto a chair in the second to last row near the door. A handful of people with cameras—reporters— were ranged along the back wall, but none of them seemed interested in my arrival.

Of course not, they were guys. And Carmen was testifying. Their eyes were glued to her.

The conversation continued up front, about how Stan wanted to date Carmen and Carmen thought Stan was a creep, while I scanned the courtroom.

The judge was sitting on the podium in the front, an older man in black robes with thinning hair. Carmen was behind another, lower podium off to the right. A court reporter sat down below on the other side, clicking away on the court record. The prosecutor must be asking the questions, because one of the two tables facing the judge and witness box was empty. At the other, I could see the backs of two heads: one slick and black, heavy on the mousse, and one wheat-colored. That one I recognized, even from this distance, as belonging to Stan Laszlo.

I wasn't prepared for the clutch in my stomach when I saw him.

It wasn't fear, exactly. He was in prison, and couldn't hurt me again. And he hadn't really hurt me the first time. I'd had a few scary minutes amid the tombstones in the old Key West Cemetery, until Ricky Fuentes showed up and arrested Stan, but I'd always known he was somewhere nearby and would come to my rescue.

And I'd gone on with life as usual the next day. I'd lost my virginity to Ty that night, and enjoyed it. I'd spent the past year talking to rape victims on the phone and in person several nights a week. I hadn't thought much about Stan, and it had never occurred to me that the attack had left any marks.

But this was the first time I'd seen him since that night, and I guess looking at him brought something to the surface I hadn't realized I had buried. I wasn't afraid, because I knew he wouldn't be able to touch me again. They'd find him guilty—because he was—and he'd spend a lot of years behind bars. But facing him from the stand tomorrow was going to be harder than I'd expected. Just looking at the back of his head was hard.

The prosecutor moved on to talking about what had happened when Carmen was raped. Since Stan had drugged her and she couldn't remember it, she wasn't able to tell him much. And that was the big problem with this trial: other than me, and one other girl he hadn't been able to dose as well as he should have because he'd already used too much of the drug on me, none of the victims remembered what had happened. Carmen hadn't even realized she'd been raped until Stan told me about it.

So my testimony, along with Ty's and Ricky Fuentes's—those of us who had actually been conscious during what happened—was pretty crucial.

Up at the front, the prosecutor finished talking to Carmen and went to sit down. Stan's lawyer bounced to his feet to cross-examine.

He started by sticking his hands in his pockets and rocking back and forth on the balls of his feet. "Miss Fuentes."

Carmen nodded.

"You're Detective Enrique Fuentes's sister, is that correct?"

"Yes," Carmen said.

"And Detective Fuentes is the officer who arrested my client last March."

"Yes," Carmen said, with a glance at her brother. He was sitting on the front row, next to a head of light brown hair that could only be Ty. They'd both been nodding occasionally, encouraging Carmen, while the prosecutor had asked her questions. A row of black heads behind them might have been the rest of the Fuenteses, come to support Carmen—and I suppose, Enrique. There were five siblings, as far as I knew, plus parents and grandparents, although I'd only met one other, Juan, before. Ricky was the eldest, Carmen the youngest, and Juan was somewhere in the middle.

The lawyer sent a significant glance toward the jury box at Carmen's admission that her brother was the arresting officer, but he didn't actually comment. Instead he asked, "Did you ever report your rape to the authorities, Miss Fuentes?"

"No," Carmen said.

"Did you tell your brother about it? Privately?

"Objection," the prosecutor said. "Asked and answered."

"Withdrawn," the defense attorney answered, as smoothly as a snake. "Why not?"

"Because until Stan was arrested, I didn't know—"

Carmen stopped talking, but by then it was too late. Stan's lawyer pounced. "You didn't know it had happened, did you?"

"No," Carmen said.

"Because at that time you were drinking heavily and partying every night and having sexual relations with numerous men, is that not correct?"

"Objection," the prosecutor shrieked, coming out of his chair, the back of his neck purple with rage. Ricky Fuentes and Ty were radiating anger, too, and the row of dark Fuentes heads turned and whispered to one another before turning as one and staring daggers at the defense attorney.

"Withdrawn," he said happily. "Nothing further."

He skipped back to his table, obviously pleased with his performance. Stan slapped him on the back, so he must be happy, too. Looked like their defense was going to be a cross between "they were asking for it because they were sluts" and "you don't remember what happened, so how do you know it actually happened?"

"Redirect?" the judge asked the prosecutor.

He said no, and the judge told Carmen she was excused. She went and sat down with her brother and Ty, who moved to the side so she could slide between them. And once she was seated, they both leaned in and started whispering encouragement to her. Meanwhile, the rest of the family leaned forward to pet and touch, too.

It was lonely here in the back of the room. I had downplayed the whole ordeal when I told my parents about it last year, and I'd made it seem like this trip to testify was no big deal, either. But now that I was here, I wasn't so sure. My mother had asked whether I wanted her to come along, but she doesn't really like to leave my father and Braxton, so I'd assured her I'd be fine on my own. I'd told her Mackenzie and Quinn would be here—neglecting to mention that they wouldn't be coming until sometime next week—and that I had friends in Key West from last time I visited. But sitting here, alone on the back row while the cameras behind me clicked and whirred and zoomed in on the back of Carmen's head and Ty's arm around her shoulders, I felt alone, like I didn't have a single friend in the whole world.

CHAPTER
Two

The trial continued with several video interviews on a screen in the front of the room. Most of the girls Stan had assaulted had been here on Spring Break, so they weren't here anymore, and they hadn't been required to come back to testify. There wasn't much they could add to what had already been said, since they didn't remember much about what happened. Stan's lawyer was a bit miffed that he wasn't given the ability to cross-examine, but the state prosecutor had made sure that each girl said she didn't remember who had given her the drugs or raped her, so the public defender pretty much got what he wanted—except for the chance to point out that the girls had been out partying, had been drunk, and had been asking for it.

It was frustrating and nauseating. The only good thing was that the girls themselves didn't hear what he was saying. They were somewhere else, going about their lives, with no idea that down here, Stan's defense attorney was doing his best to smear their reputations and make it seem like Stan had just taken what they'd offered.

But that would change tomorrow. Other than Carmen, who was local and convenient, and who could add some background on Stan's motivations, there were two of us who had actually made the trip to Key West to testify. Me, and the girl Stan had attacked the night he'd had me and then lost me. I'd run into her in the hospital the next day, and the poor thing had looked awful, all beaten and bruised. But she remembered things. And of course I did, too. So between the two of us, and Ty and Ricky Fuentes, there was plenty of testimony to put Stan away. No matter what Stan's lawyer said or did.

Court adjourned for the day just before five. I stayed in my seat and watched while two uniformed cops put handcuffs on Stan and took him away, back to jail. Carmen, Ty, and Ricky Fuentes got up, followed by the rest of the Fuentes clan, and filed out. None of them looked at me. Not even Ty. He was too busy murmuring sweet nothings in Carmen's ear. She had paired that prim white blouse with a black skirt that reached to her knees, but which was so tight it was a miracle she could walk. They minced out the door at a snail's pace, with Carmen's booty swaying under the black fabric.

I was about to get up and head toward the front when I heard a voice. "Cassie!" Juan must have noticed me sitting here, because he made a detour in my direction.

"Nice to see you," I said.

"We're going to my mom's house for dinner. You wanna come?"

And watch Ty hand-feed Carmen morsels of food? No thanks.

"I should go introduce myself to the prosecutor," I said, and tried to sound like I regretted not being able to take him up on the invitation. "I just got here this afternoon. And we haven't spoken yet. Other than on the phone, I mean. But he'll probably want to talk to me in person now that I'm here."

Juan nodded. "You're testifying tomorrow?"

I told him I was, if everything had gone according to

schedule. Up at the front of the room, the prosecutor finished putting legal pads and pencils into his briefcase and reached for the jacket hanging on the back of his chair.

"Go," Juan said. "We'll probably be at Captain Crow's tonight, if you wanna stop by."

"Captain Crow's? Not Captain Tony's?"

Juan works at Captain Tony's. While Captain Crow's is where Mackenzie, Quinn and I spent most of our time during Spring Break last year. Mackenzie's Austin tended bar there, and Quinn's James had occupied a corner with his buddies, tossing back shots of Tequila.

And it was where I'd met Ty.

"Captain Crow's," Juan said, already on his way toward the door, hustling to catch up to the rest of his family. "See you."

He was already gone, so there was no point in telling him I probably wouldn't show up. Seeing Ty from a distance had been difficult enough. Having to deal with him would be worse. Especially at Captain Crow's. And especially with the way he was slobbering all over Carmen.

But there'd be time to make that decision later. Right now, I had to catch the prosecutor before he left.

I scurried to the front of the room and stopped him just as he turned toward the door. By now the room was mostly empty. I introduced myself—"I'm Cassie Wilder. We've spoken on the phone,"—and waited.

"Cassie!" He perked right up. "We need to talk. Have you eaten?"

"A hot dog for lunch," I said.

"Let's go grab some dinner." He took his briefcase in one hand and my elbow in the other and headed for the door. Stan's attorney, who was still standing at the next table shoveling things into his briefcase, watched us go with a calculating look on his face.

"I don't like that man," I told the prosecutor when we were out in the hallway.

He glanced over his shoulder. "He's just doing his job."

"I wouldn't want his job."

He let go of my elbow and just walked beside me as we approached the double doors to the outside. The security guard was standing beside them, probably ready to start closing up shop for the day once all the stragglers had left the building.

"I'm sure he doesn't want it either," the prosecutor said. "But everyone is entitled to counsel. People who can't afford to hire their own, get a public defender appointed to them."

"I don't have a problem with that." Of course everyone is entitled to legal representation. It's a basic right. "I just don't like this guy's attitude. It seems like he's trying to make all the girls look like—"

At the last minute I edited out the word *sluts* and substituted, "like they were asking for it."

"He's doing his job," the prosecutor maintained, nodding to the security guard on our way past. "See you, Don."

"Have a good evening, Mr. DeWitt," the security guard answered. "Miss Wilder." He nodded to me.

We walked outside with the prosecutor telling me, "He's right, you know."

"The defense attorney?" How could he say that? And how could he possibly prosecute Stan if that's what he thought?

"They don't know that the defendant raped them," the prosecutor said. "Aside from you and Paula, nobody can identify him."

"But that's not their fault! He drugged them."

"And we'll get him for it. But it's the public defender's job to make the defendant look as innocent as possible. And if he can knock a couple of the assault charges off the table, because we can't prove that the defendant actually raped some of the girls, he's doing his job."

He shook his head. "We all want Laszlo to pay. We all want him put in a cage for as long as possible. But he's entitled to have someone point out all the holes in the prosecution's case, and that's a big hole. I'm not very happy with the tactic opposing counsel has chosen myself, but he's entitled to structure his case as he sees fit."

I supposed. "There's no question that Stan will be found guilty, right?"

"There's always a question," the prosecutor told me. "But in my more than twenty years on the job, I've never had a more air-tight case than this one."

He smiled. "So where would you like to eat?"

We ended up at an Italian restaurant, where we spent several hours going over what would happen tomorrow, and my testimony. He told me what he planned to ask me, and I gave him the answers I'd be giving when he did. And he warned me about the kinds of questions I could expect to hear during the cross-examination, which I had already figured out on my own. We went over those, too, and even though I knew I had done nothing wrong and was not to blame for what Stan did, I could still feel myself blush at some of the things he asked.

"Wear a pretty summer dress tomorrow," he told me when we parted ways outside the restaurant just before eight. "Something that makes you look young and sweet."

"I *am* young and sweet," I said. "So you don't want me to wear what Carmen wore?"

"No." He shook his head. "God, no. With Carmen, we were trying to play down her sex appeal. She's a stunner, and I knew the defense would try to paint her as a tramp. I didn't want the jury to see her that way. So we did our best to tone her down. I'm not sure how well it worked." He grimaced.

"I imagine she'd be hard to tone down," I told him, as envy curled through my stomach.

"But I want you to look like the girl next door. Young and sweet and innocent."

Like a preacher's daughter. *Check*. "I can do that," I said. "Be sure to ask me about my parents and my sex life up to last year's Spring Break. I'll try not to blush on the stand."

"Oh, no." The prosecutor shook his head. "You blush as

much as you want, Cassie. As much as you want."

Right. Young and sweet and innocent.

He looked around, at the streets teeming with tourists and those college students who had Spring Break a week earlier than me. Next week would be insane; this week was merely crazy. "Do you want me to walk you home?"

"I'm good," I said. "Juan Fuentes told me they're hanging out at Captain Crow's tonight. I think I might stop by before I go back to the motel."

He nodded. "Make sure you get home safe. Take a cab or get someone to walk with you. These streets can be crazy. No one knows that better than you."

Exactly. "I'll be careful."

"See you tomorrow. We start at nine o'clock sharp. I'll expect you there at eight forty-five."

I told him I'd be there and watched him walk off in one direction, briefcase swinging, before I turned in the other.

Here's the thing: I was going to have to face Ty in court tomorrow. He may not have noticed me today, hiding in the back, but tomorrow I'd be on the witness stand, and he'd be there on the first row. I wouldn't be able to avoid him. So maybe it would be easier to deal with it now, in private—or semi-private—instead of tomorrow, in front of the full court, with judge and jury, cameras, reporters, and all.

Besides, he might not even be at Captain Crow's. He and Carmen might have gone somewhere else. Maybe it would be just Juan at the bar. And I could ask him whether Ty and Carmen were officially involved, or whether it just looked that way.

The Italian restaurant was just a couple of blocks from Captain Crow's, so the trip didn't take long. When I pushed the door open and walked in, it was like *déjà vu* all over again: like it was last year, and I'd see Mackenzie talking to Austin at the bar, and James staring at Quinn from the table in the corner.

But of course it wasn't: Barry, the bartender from last year, was talking to Juan Fuentes, and the table in the corner was occupied by Ty and Carmen, who didn't look up at all when I walked in.

I ignored them, and headed for the bar. "Hi." I slid up on the stool next to Juan.

"Cassie." He smiled. "Something to drink?"

"Just a Sprite, please." I'd learned my lesson about getting impaired. Sometimes the nice guy who offers to see you safely home, isn't such a nice guy after all.

In a perfect world, we'd all be able to do whatever we wanted whenever we wanted to, and without having to worry about the consequences. But the world we live in is far from perfect, and I've learned that I'm safer if I take certain precautions. Like staying mostly sober and not wandering the streets alone at night.

And no, I'm not saying that just because a girl is impaired and wearing a shirt that says *Save a Virgin – Do Me Instead*, she's asking to be raped. She's not. And any man who rapes her, is still guilty of rape, no matter what she was wearing or what he thought when he looked at her. But I do think we need to take some responsibility for the situations we put ourselves in. If I get in a cage with a tiger and the tiger eats me, it isn't the tiger's fault. It's mine. The tiger's just being a tiger, and I should have stayed out of its cage. And while a man isn't a tiger and should behave better, that's still no reason to act stupidly. Sometimes, bad things happen to people who aren't careful. So I try to be careful so they won't happen to me. Doesn't mean I'm trying to excuse what Stan did—I hoped he'd spend the rest of his life in prison, with bad dreams every night—but we live in a fallen world (as my father would say), and behaving like the world is perfect and full of only nice people, is dangerous.

So I was drinking Sprite. Barry put the glass in front of me on the counter and went off to take care of other customers. I turned to Juan. "So."

"So?"

"How long has that been going on?"

"That?"

"The two of them." I nodded toward the corner, where Ty and Carmen had their heads together.

"I don't see anything going on," Juan said, taking a sip of his drink. It was pale green and looked like a slushy, but was probably a Margarita or something.

"They look chummy."

"They were chummy last year, too."

"Yes," I said, "but then Carmen was Ty's liaison with your brother and the police. He's not undercover now."

And then I thought about it. "He isn't, is he?"

Juan shook his head. "He's just here for the trial, same as you."

Right. I took another sip of Sprite. "So there's nothing going on?"

"Nope," Juan said. And added, "Last year, I assumed you and Ty would end up together."

Me, too.

"We did," I said. "For a while."

Juan looked at me, a tiny wrinkle between his brows.

He's a good-looking guy: twenty-six maybe, with the same big, brown eyes and curly, black hair as his sister. She keeps hers long, Juan keeps his short. He looks like a younger, prettier version of Enrique, all smooth golden skin and white teeth, with a stud in one ear. The white jeans he had changed into were tight enough to show off a very nice butt he was currently sitting on, and the turquoise polo-shirt clung tight to his biceps and chest.

He caught me looking and flashed a grin.

"Sorry," I said.

"No problem. So what happened?"

I sighed and turned my attention back to reality. "With Ty? He kept disappearing. Things were great when he was around, but every few weeks he'd get sent out on another undercover assignment. He couldn't tell me where he was going or what he was doing. He couldn't contact me while he was gone. And he couldn't talk about it when he got back. So I spent half my time worrying that he was dead, and the other half worrying about when he was leaving again."

"Being involved with someone in law enforcement is hard," Juan said, sipping his drink. "Enrique just sticks around Key West, it's not like he disappears for days and weeks at a time, but every time he straps on a weapon, we all know there's a chance he'll run into trouble and won't come back home."

I nodded. "I managed to keep it together for six months. We broke up the day before Thanksgiving. I haven't spoken to him since."

I shot another glance over into the corner, where Ty and Carmen were leaning toward one another. She whispered in his ear, and I felt my eyes narrow.

Mine!

Except he wasn't. Not anymore. And I was the one who had broken up with him, so I had only myself to blame.

"I don't suppose you want to be my boyfriend?" I asked Juan wistfully. A nice, safe bartender, one who stayed in one place and didn't go off on missions to save the world, was just what I needed.

He looked at me like I'd lost my mind. I guess that was probably a no.

"Or maybe you can just pretend to be my boyfriend." That way, it would look like I had moved on, too. Like I wasn't sitting over here watching every move Ty and Carmen made.

Juan grinned. "It isn't that I don't appreciate the offer, *querida*. I guess nobody told you I bat for the other team?"

I blinked at him. What other team?

"I'm gay," Juan said.

"Oh." I blushed. "I'm sorry. No, nobody mentioned that."

"No reason why they would," Juan said easily. "So while I like you, I don't wanna sleep with you. Or pretend I'm sleeping with you."

"Of course not." *Gah*.

"Besides, I'm pretty sure Carmen knows. Ty probably

does, too."

Probably. He was much better than me at picking up on subtle clues like that.

Not that this one had been all that subtle. Juan had pretty much had to hit me over the head with it.

"Sorry," I said.

"No problem. I'm flattered you asked."

Sure. "I'm just going to go," I said and slid off the stool. "I've been stupid enough for one night. And I don't want to sit here and watch them any longer."

Juan glanced over into the corner and then at his watch. "I'll walk you back to your hotel. I have to cut out soon in any case." He left enough money on the counter to cover his drink and my Sprite, in spite of my offers to pay for my own. "C'mon."

He put his hand on my lower back on the way to the door. I didn't look back as we exited, but it probably didn't matter, anyway. Ty wouldn't be watching.

CHAPTER

Three

"Hot date?" I asked Juan as we walked down Duval in the direction of Richardson's.

He glanced over. He wasn't all that much taller than me. Ty's height, more or less. Five-ten or so. "Scuse me?"

"You said you had to cut out soon in any case. Are you meeting someone?"

"Oh." He smiled faintly. "Yeah. I'm not sure it's a date, though. Especially not a hot one. But yeah, I'm meeting someone."

"I'll be OK on my own," I said, "if it's going to be a problem for you to walk me to the motel and get back in time."

He shook his head. "It's not. And besides, Enrique would have my head if I let you walk alone."

"I could take a cab."

"It's just a few minutes," Juan said and changed the subject. "So are you nervous about tomorrow?"

We spent the rest of the walk talking about the trial and what the prosecutor had told me to expect in the morning. I told Juan of my impression that the public defender was going out of his way to make all the victims seem like tramps, and he nodded, his handsome face darkening. "That's the reason a lot of women never report rapes, you know. Court turns into a circus where the victims are on trial as much as the rapist."

I nodded. "It's awful. Bad enough to be assaulted in the first place, but then to have to deal with a second sort of assault to prove that the guy who raped you really did rape you, and you didn't do anything to encourage it—"

"You'll be OK," Juan told me. "You're strong. I'm more worried about the other girl."

"Paula."

He nodded. "What she went through was terrible. And she's very brave to come back to testify."

Yes, she was. Stan hadn't harmed me. He'd beaten and raped her. And if I felt a twinge of unease about facing him in court tomorrow, I could only imagine what she must be feeling. "I'll try to talk to her," I said. "I've spent the past year volunteering at a rape hotline. I've talked to a lot of girls who've been assaulted. I've gotten better at knowing what to say."

Juan nodded.

"Will you be there tomorrow?"

"I'll try to be. At least in the morning. I have to go in to work in the afternoon, so I can't stay all day, but I'll be there for a little bit."

"Thank you," I said, happy that at least there'd be one friendly face in the room when I took the stand.

We walked me to the front entrance to the motel and stopped, because I did. "You gonna be OK from here?"

"I'm sure," I said, since I'd noticed him looking at his watch a couple of times on the walk. "I'm sorry if I've kept you too long."

"Not a problem." He flashed a smile. "You sure you don't want me to come inside and check under the bed before I go?"

"It's a platform. Nowhere for anyone to hide underneath.

There's no proper closet, and if anyone's hiding behind the shower curtain, I'll bludgeon him with my curling iron. Just go, so you're not late." The last thing I wanted was to screw up Juan's love life. Bad enough how thoroughly I had screwed up my own.

He nodded. "I'll see you in court tomorrow, then."

I said he would, and then I watched him turn and walk away—his white jeans like a beacon in the dark—for a few seconds before I turned toward the motel.

The office was closed for the night, but this was Key West, so the pool was still open and people were still lounging and splashing. The sun had set at least an hour ago, but the pavement still held the heat, and the air was still warm. I walked to my door, fumbling my key out of my purse, and inserted it in the lock. Each unit had its own little light above the door, so I had no problem seeing what I was doing. And because I'd realized I might be back late, I had kept the bathroom light on when I left. The bedroom was empty, nobody was lying in wait to attack me, and the shower curtain was pulled back and the shower empty. I didn't need to use the curling iron.

I took my makeup and clothes off, brushed my teeth, and spent a little time reading. And then, when it got quiet outside, I turned the lights off and went to sleep. The more I thought about it, the larger tomorrow's ordeal was looming in my mind, and I figured the best thing I could do was just stop thinking about it for a while.

I had set the alarm to go off early so I'd have plenty of time to get ready and to the Courthouse by eight forty-five. And because I was nervous, I woke up before the alarm and lay there for a while, staring up at the ceiling in the dark, waiting for the sound.

My stomach was churning too much for breakfast, so after I showered and dressed—demurely, as ordered, in a white eyelet dress with a full skirt—I tucked my still-damp hair behind my ears, left most of my makeup off, and started walking to the Courthouse.

I wasn't the first witness of the day, and when I got there, to the little anteroom where the prosecutor had told me to report for duty, I found him at a table, busy talking to Paula, the girl who had run afoul Stan on the night when he'd tried and failed to hold on to me.

Like me—like all the girls Stan had attacked last year—she looked sweet and innocent. Long, blond hair, big, blue eyes, demure dress. Unlike me, she was crying, shaking her head back and forth. "I can't do this. I can't face him."

The prosecutor was patting her hand, telling her he had faith in her and she could do it, while a middle-aged woman—Paula's mother, I assumed—hovered a few yards away, looking uncertain.

When I walked in, they all turned to me.

I blinked. "Hi. I'm Cassie Wilder."

The prosecutor straightened. He looked relieved. "Cassie is testifying today, too."

Paula looked at me. So did her mother.

"Remember everything we talked about?" the prosecutor asked me.

I nodded. "I'm ready." Or as ready as I'd ever be. "Ready to get it over with," I added, as much to make Paula feel better—we were in the same boat here—as because it was the truth.

"You were in the hospital," Paula said.

"Yes. I was."

"When I was there."

"Yes. I was." I had seen her. I hadn't realized she'd seen me. At that point, I hadn't thought she'd been aware of anything outside herself and her nightmares.

"Did he drug you too?"

I nodded. He had, yes. Drugged me, and then lost me, and then taken his frustration out on her.

"We're not going to think about that now," the prosecutor said firmly. "We'll talk about it on the stand. You'll testify, and then you'll go sit down. Or leave, if you prefer. And Cassie will testify. And then we'll all go have lunch and celebrate that we're here and he's in jail."

Sounded good to me. Something nice to look forward to. Not only was I not going to enjoy delivering my own testimony, but I would have to sit and listen to Paula go into detail about what had happened to her, too, with the knowledge that it had been my fault.

Or not my fault, exactly, but if Stan had been able to hang on to me that night, Paula wouldn't have been attacked, and wouldn't have to be here now.

Then again, if Stan had been able to hang on to me that night, I wouldn't have been in a position to help Enrique and Ty catch him two days later, so maybe it had all worked out the way it was supposed to.

"I want the two of you to wait here until the bailiff comes and gets you," the prosecutor told us. "Mrs. Carlson," he looked at Paula's mom, "you may choose to stay here with your daughter, or come to the courtroom with me. She's our first witness of the day, so it doesn't matter either way."

"In that case I'll come with you," Mrs. Carlson said, "and find a seat. If that's OK with you, Paula?"

Paula swallowed, but nodded.

"We'll be OK here on our own," I said.

So the prosecutor left and took Mrs. Carlson with him. Paula and I looked at one another.

"We're going to be OK," I told her. "It's going to be hard, and scary, and we'll have to look at him, but we'll get through it. And then he'll go to prison and we'll go home."

She nodded, and took a shuddering sort of breath. "Where are you from?"

I told her I'd grown up in a small town in the middle of nowhere, Ohio, but that I went to the University of Chicago. "You?"

"Wisconsin," Paula said. "Nursing school."

"I was studying English. But I switched to journalism this year."

"Because of what happened?"

I nodded. "I wrote a couple of articles about it, for the school newspaper. It helped. Me, and the girls who read them. So I thought maybe that was something I could do. To help. Become a journalist. And write about the bad stuff."

Paula nodded. "That's what I want to do, too. Help."

"And you will. We'll go out there and tell the jury what happened, and we'll help put him away. And then we'll go have ice cream or something. I'll need ice cream after that."

Paula smiled, the first smile I'd seen so far. "I wouldn't mind some ice cream."

"It's a date," I said. "You and me and your mom and the prosecutor."

I held out my hand. She took it, and we sat there together and waited to be called into the courtroom.

The prosecutor did things in chronological order, so Paula went first. I went into the courtroom with her, because I thought it might encourage her. I held her hand until we got to the front of the room, and while she went up to the witness box, I took a seat at the prosecution's table. I didn't look around, and I certainly didn't glance over at Stan. I'd have to look at him later, when it was my turn to testify, and that would be soon enough.

Paula put her hand on the Bible the bailiff held up, and promised to tell the truth. Then she sat down behind the microphone and twisted her hands together in her lap.

The next ninety minutes are some of the longest of my life. Wrestling with Stan on the ground at the Key West Cemetery, feeling him tugging at my clothes and wrapping his hands around my throat, was pretty bad. Breaking up with Ty was awful. But listening to Paula's voice shake as she recalled her encounter with Stan a year ago, hearing her describe the things he said and the things he did, the names he called her, the impact of his fists hitting her face... that was agonizing. I've never been so glad for anything to be over as when the prosecutor said he had no further questions.

And then he turned to Lew Berryman, the public defender. "Your witness, counselor."

I braced myself, and saw Paula do the same. Behind me, I heard a sniff from Mrs. Carlson. I think we were all blown away when Berryman said, "No questions."

The judge nodded to Paula. "You may step down, Ms. Carlson. Thank you for your testimony."

Paula got to her feet and executed a tiny curtsey. Either that, or she found herself weak in the knees. "Thank you." She scurried out of the witness box and across the floor.

"Call your next witness, Mr. DeWitt," the judge told the prosecutor, who gave me the eye and a tiny nod.

"The state calls Cassandra Wilder, Your Honor."

I got up, noticing I was a little weak in the knees myself. But Paula had gotten through it, with a harder story to share than the one I had. How could I do less?

I made it across the floor and into the witness box. The bailiff brought the Bible again, and I put my hand on it and promised to tell the truth, the whole truth, and nothing but the truth, so help me God.

And then I sat down and folded my hands in my lap and waited.

Mr. DeWitt got to his feet. "Where are you from, Ms. Wilder?"

I told him I was born in Braxton, Ohio. "But I came here from Chicago. I attend UC."

"But your parents live in Braxton? What does your father do for a living?"

"He's a minister," I said.

"So you're a preacher's daughter." He sent a significant look toward the jury, to make sure they understood this very important point. I was a nice girl. I was brought up to tell the truth. They could trust me.

"Yes, sir." I did my best to look like my father's daughter.

"And your mother?"

31

"She's the minister's wife. She takes care of my father, and helps him write his sermons, and ministers to the congregation, and teaches Sunday School..."

"And did you teach Sunday School, Ms. Wilder?"

"Every Sunday until I went to college," I said.

Mr. DeWitt smiled, pleased. "Tell us about the first time you visited Key West, Ms. Wilder."

"It was for Spring Break last year," I said. "I came down with two friends and stayed a week."

"And during the course of this week, you had occasion to cross paths with the defendant, Stanley Laszlo."

I hadn't looked at Stan yet. Now I did, with my heart thudding a little harder in my chest than usual. "Yes, sir."

He looked the same. Maybe a little older, like a year in prison hadn't agreed with him. Ty had told me Stan hadn't been able to make bail, so I knew he'd spent the past year behind bars. And former cops don't have an easy time of it when they have to mingle with criminals. Even when they're criminals themselves.

But for the most part he looked like he had a year ago. Small head on a long neck, with a beaky nose and blue eyes that were fastened on me. When I looked at him, he smirked.

Smirked.

I looked away, like it didn't bother me, although it did. He had no right to smirk. After what he'd done, he had no right to sit there and make those of us who were testifying against him feel uncomfortable.

The courtroom was pretty full today, too. There were reporters with cameras along the back wall again. They'd been warned not to take pictures of Paula, since she was a rape victim and had a right to privacy, but I wasn't, so every once in a while, I heard the click of a shutter or the whirring of a lens.

The Fuenteses were absent today, of course. Their daughter wasn't testifying. And Juan wasn't here, either. I was a little bummed about that. It would have been nice to see a friendly face. Although the fact that Juan hadn't bothered to show up was soon lost in the shock of the next realization: Ty wasn't here, either. Nor, for that matter, was Enrique Fuentes, although I didn't really care about that. I was a little surprised, granted. He was the arresting officer. He'd have to testify, although probably not today. But I'd have thought he'd want to attend the whole trial.

But Ty...

He'd been here for Carmen's testimony yesterday. He'd touched her and encouraged her and told her what a good job she'd done when it was over.

But when it was my turn, he couldn't even bother to show up?

"Ms. Wilder?" the prosecutor said.

I came back to myself. "I'm sorry. Could you repeat the question?"

He had a little wrinkle between his brows. "We were talking about the first time you made Mr. Laszlo's acquaintance. Can you remember?"

"Of course." I yanked my mind back on track. Ty could wait. What mattered now was making sure Stan Laszlo never saw daylight again. "The first time I saw Officer Laszlo was my second night here. He was standing on the corner down the street from Captain Crow's Bar on Duval when Agent Connor was walking me home."

"And he saw you?"

"Agent Connor said hello to him," I said. "So yes, he did."

"He saw you together."

I nodded. "Yes, he did."

And it went on from there. How I'd found the first victim of last year's Spring Break on the beach the next morning: a girl named Elizabeth, who'd been wearing a pink dress like the one I'd worn the night before, and who had long blond hair a lot like mine.

The testimony seemed to go on forever. The prosecutor was very carefully building his case, from Stan to me to Ty. Or from me to Ty to Stan. Either way. The point being that Stan had targeted me specifically because of Ty. It was a damned shame that Ty wasn't here, because the visual aid—for the jury, I mean—would have been helpful.

We moved past Stan drugging me the first time on Tuesday night and losing me to Ty when the latter came across him 'helping' me down the street.

"Tell us what happened the next day."

Sure. I talked about waking up and not remembering anything. About going to the hospital and being examined. About seeing Paula there, and the condition she'd been in. My voice started to shake, and Stan smirked again.

"You don't have to go into detail about Ms. Carlson's condition," the prosecutor told me. "We'll be hearing from Dr. Johnson later this afternoon, and she will cover the medical evidence. Did you see the defendant on Wednesday?"

I hadn't. I'd spent the afternoon at the clinic, and the evening in the hotel, having dinner with Ty. That's when he'd told me about being an FBI agent and why my crush on him wasn't going to go anywhere.

"Tell us what happened on Thursday," Mr. DeWitt said.

"I spent the day with Agent Connor. We went sightseeing."

"And in the evening?"

"We went to Captain Crow's," I said, "and pretended to argue, so I could storm out of there alone and hopefully draw Mr. Laszlo's attention."

"Objection," Mr. Berryman said.

"Sustained," the judge agreed. "The jury will disregard the use of the defendant's name. Ms. Wilder..."

"Yes, Your Honor. I left the bar alone, hoping to draw the rapist's attention, since we believed he'd come after me."

The judge nodded, pleased.

"At that point," Mr. DeWitt wanted to know, "did you suspect the defendant?"

"I didn't. And if Ty... Agent Connor did, he didn't mention it."

Mr. DeWitt nodded. "What happened then?"

What happened then was that I'd run into Stan, who was standing outside the Key West Cemetery. And since I'd had no idea he was the man I was looking for, I hadn't realized that going into the cemetery with him was a bad idea.

"He told me he just wanted to protect me," I said. "Instead, he attacked me. I tried to fight him off, and eventually Detective Fuentes showed up and arrested him."

"And while you were talking, he confessed to you," Mr. DeWitt said.

I nodded. "Yes, he did. He told me all about what he'd done, and why, and how."

"Why would he do that, Ms. Wilder?"

"I think he was planning to kill me," I said.

"Objection!" The defense attorney was on his feet. "Move to strike. My client is not charged with attempted murder!"

The judge hesitated. "I'll let it stand," he said eventually. "But the jury is to keep in mind that the defendant is charged with assault, rape, and attempted rape, not murder."

The jury nodded.

The judge turned to the prosecutor. "Anything further for this witness, Mr. DeWitt?"

"No," Mr. DeWitt said, with satisfaction, "I think that should do it."

"Cross, Mr. Berryman?"

"Don't mind if I do," Berryman said, bounding to his feet. "Ms. Wilder."

I nodded.

"What precisely is your relationship with Agent Connor?"

"Objection," Mr. DeWitt said, but without much enthusiasm.

"I don't mind," I told him, and turned back to Mr. Berryman. "We don't have a relationship."

"At the time, did you have a relationship?"

I shook my head.

"Out loud, for the record," the judge reminded me.

"No, we did not have a relationship. We were friendly. I

liked him. But I knew he was working undercover and that getting romantically involved was not an option. So we had no relationship."

The defense attorney looked frustrated. "Did Agent Connor spend the night in your room on Tuesday, March 18th of last year?"

"I believe he did," I said. "He said he did. But since I was under the influence of your client's drugs, I can't really say for certain."

Berryman looked like he was thinking of objecting to my fingering his client, but he had bigger fish to fry. "So it's possible Agent Connor spent the night in your room and you had sexual relations."

"No," I said, "that's not possible."

"But you just said you don't remember what happened."

"I know what didn't. I went to the hospital the next day to be examined. And I was still a virgin."

There was a titter throughout the room. Not quite a whisper, not quite a giggle. A few of the cameras clicked and whirred.

"You were a virgin," Mr. Berryman said blankly.

I nodded, and then remembered the court reporter. "Yes. Both before and after Agent Connor spent the night in my room." And both before and after my encounter with Stan in the cemetery.

It was kind of funny, to be honest. Last year, the fact that I was a 21-year-old virgin hadn't been information I wanted to spread around. It was embarrassing. I'd been certain I was the only 21-year-old virgin in Key West. But this year I had no problem admitting it.

Maybe it was because I wasn't a virgin anymore, so I didn't feel quite so stigmatized. Or maybe I'd just gotten over thinking I was all that special. Either way, throwing last year's status in Mr. Berryman's face felt pretty good. *Hi, I'm Cassie Wilder, and I was a virgin until I was twenty-one.*

"Anything further, Mr. Berryman?" the judge prompted

when the public defender didn't speak.

Berryman shook his head. "But I reserve the right to recall this witness, Your Honor."

"So noted," the judge said and glanced at his watch. "Let's adjourn for lunch. We'll start again at two o'clock."

"All rise," the bailiff said.

We rose. The judge swept out in a swirl of black robes, the uniformed officers came to take Stan to his bread and water, and Mr. DeWitt turned to me. "Well done, Cassie. Let's go celebrate."

CHAPTER
Four

$\mathscr{T}$echnically, it may have been a little early to celebrate. There were several witnesses yet to go for the prosecution, and then whatever case the defense had built. I couldn't imagine that Stan wouldn't be found guilty, though. There were enough of us who had seen him in the act that he shouldn't be able to wiggle out of it.

The prosecutor shook his head when I said so. "We'll get him."

"You don't think they'll pull out some ridiculous defense at the last minute, that'll sway the jury?"

"I can't imagine what," Mr. DeWitt said. "He was methodical and controlled in what he did, so there's no question of diminished capacity. And Detective Fuentes caught him red-handed."

"He can't—I don't know—call it entrapment, or anything?"

Mr. DeWitt shook his head. "You didn't force him to attack you. If I understand the situation right, you didn't even suspect him."

"I didn't. He was a cop. I assumed the cops were the good guys."

"As one should," Mr. DeWitt said.

And as one can't always, unfortunately.

"Will you be staying in Key West now that your testimony is done?" Mrs. Carlson asked me. She and Paula had come to lunch with us, too. Paula looked a little pale and tired, but also relieved that it was over. And unlike me, the public defender hadn't reserved the right to recall her. Probably didn't want to risk her saying anything else that would make his client look even more like a monster.

I nodded. "He might call me back for another round. And I want to be here for the verdict, anyway. Besides, our Spring Break is next week. I'm meeting some friends."

"You said you were here with Mackenzie Forbes last year," Paula said.

I nodded.

"I just love her!"

You and most of the rest of the country. Mac wasn't dubbed America's Country Sweetheart for nothing. And it had been interesting to see America's reaction to her tattooed and not-at-all-sweet boyfriend.

"She'll be here next week," I said. "Her boyfriend's from Key West. He was tending bar at Captain Crow's last year. You probably met him."

"Austin?" Paula asked. I nodded. "Wow. And now he's dating Mackenzie Forbes!"

Yes, indeed.

Paula turned to look at her mother. Mrs. Carlson sighed. "I guess we could stay a little longer. I thought you wanted to leave, though."

"That was before I knew Mackenzie Forbes was coming," Paula said. "And I kind of want to be here for the verdict, too. I want to see him go to jail for a long time."

Mrs. Carlson hesitated. "I'll call your father and talk to him," she said eventually. I don't think it was a firm yes, but

Paula knew her mother better than I did, and Paula seemed pleased, so maybe it would work out. And anyway, after what she'd been through—both last year and on the witness stand today—she deserved a special treat. Something more than ice cream.

"I'll check with Mackenzie and find out when she's getting here," I said and pulled out my phone. "Maybe we can all go get a drink or something."

Paula looked like I had offered her rather more than a chance to watch Mackenzie Forbes suck down Sex on the Beach. "God, I'd love that!"

"Give me your number. I'll text you when I know something."

She rattled it off and I saved it in my contacts. I was putting the phone back in my bag when it rang.

At first I thought I might have accidentally pushed a button and gotten my ringtone. But no, there was an actual number on my screen. Local, and not one I recognized.

I put the phone to my ear. "Hello?"

"Cassandra Wilder?" a female voice said. "This is the Key West Police."

Uh-oh. "Something wrong?"

"An accident," the voice said. "Detective Fuentes told me to call you and ask you to come in to see him."

Accident?

All the air left my body, and I had a hard time catching my breath. "Agent Connor?" I managed. "Is Agent Connor OK?"

"Yes, miss," the voice said. "He's here, too."

Thank you, God.

I told her I was on my way and turned to Mr. DeWitt. "The police want to see me. Do you have any idea what that might be about?"

Mr. DeWitt shook his head. "If something was going on with the trial, they'd have called me, too. Must be something else."

Must be. "I'll come to the Courthouse later," I said. "After

I've done whatever Ricky Fuentes wants. Maybe he just wants a rundown on what happened in court this morning. Or he wants to explain why he and Agent Connor couldn't make it today."

Because frankly, I thought I deserved an explanation for that.

Mr. DeWitt nodded. "We'll see you this afternoon."

The three of them settled in to have dessert—ice cream—and I grabbed my purse and headed out.

I'd been to the Key West police headquarters last year, of course. They were located about midway across the island, near the Palm Avenue Causeway: a mile, mile-and-a-half from the restaurant. I got there with no problems, and asked for Enrique Fuentes. After a couple of minutes, Ricky showed up to take me to his office.

He looked terrible, like he hadn't slept much last night.

"Goodness," I said, "what happened to you?"

He glanced down at me. He's an older, grimmer, slightly taller and harder version of his brother, with the same curly black hair and brown eyes. But where Juan's eyes are like melting chocolate, Enrique's are more like stone. "Nothing happened to me."

I don't think I imagined the emphasis on the pronoun. "Who, then?"

"My brother," Ricky said.

"Juan?" I stopped dead in the middle of the Key West Police bullpen, with cops in cubicles all around me. "Something happened to Juan?"

"We'll talk in my office," Ricky said and took my arm.

I let him escort me into his office—roughly the size of one of the cubicles outside, just more private—and sat down in the chair he indicated. "What happened to Juan? I saw him just last night."

"I know," Enrique said, walking around the desk to take a seat. "That's why I want to talk to you."

The other visitor's chair was occupied by my former boyfriend, and under the circumstances, my heart hardly skipped a beat at seeing him. He didn't pay much attention to me, either, just looked up from his cell phone, where he was busy manipulating keys, and nodded before going back to what he was doing.

I did my best to ignore him. "What happened to Juan?"

"He's in the hospital," Ricky said. "In an induced coma. Someone attacked him last night. I need you to tell me everything that happened."

I could feel myself turn pale, and did my best to focus. "Nothing happened. I stopped by the Courthouse and caught the last hour or two of testimony yesterday. A little of Carmen's, and then the video interviews. Juan told me you were all going to have dinner together and invited me to come along, but I had to introduce myself to Mr. DeWitt, and I had dinner with him. After that I went to Captain Crow's, because Juan had said you'd be there. You weren't—"

Ricky Fuentes shook his head.

"But Ty and Carmen were. And Juan. I sat at the bar and had a glass of Sprite, and then Juan walked me home."

"Where are you staying?"

I told him I had booked a room at Richardson's Motel. I sensed, or saw out of the corner of my eye, Ty looking up at me, but I didn't turn my head.

"Did he come in with you?" Ricky wanted to know.

I shook my head. "He left me at the entrance. There were still people in the pool, and he was in a hurry."

"Did he tell you who he was meeting?"

Whom. Former English major; what can I say?

"No," I said. "I asked if he had a hot date, and he said he didn't know if he'd call it a date, let alone a hot one. But that he was meeting someone."

"Did he say where?"

No, he hadn't told me that, either.

"Anything else you can think of, that might help?"

I shrugged, helplessly. "He looked like he'd dressed up. White jeans and a turquoise shirt. Like he hoped to make a good impression. But he didn't say anything more about him. We talked about the trial, mostly. And... um..."

"Um?" Enrique said, arching his brows.

I slid my gaze sideways. "Ty. And what went wrong."

"What went wrong?" Enrique said.

I nodded to Ty. "Ask him."

Enrique turned to Ty, who told him, "Didn't we already talk about this? It's tough, being involved with someone in law enforcement."

I nodded. Even Juan had said so. "I'm sorry I can't be more help. But he really didn't say much. Can you tell me what happened?"

"He was found this morning," Enrique said, his lips tight, "in the cemetery."

I blinked. "The old Key West cemetery? But..."

Enrique nodded, his face grim. There was no need to spell out that the old Key West Cemetery was where Stan had attacked me, as well as a girl named Jeanine, last year.

"Coincidence?" I asked.

"Hard to see how it could be anything else. Stan's in jail, and he never went for men, anyway. But we're keeping our options open."

"Was Juan... um...?"

"No," Ty said, as Enrique's face congealed. "No sexual assault. He was just beaten badly and knocked out. The doctor put him under so he can get some rest. Carmen's sitting with him. And he has a guard on the door."

His voice didn't change when he said Carmen's name. His face didn't, either. Under the circumstances, I probably shouldn't be happy about that, but a shameful little part of me was.

"We're pulling video feeds from any cameras near the cemetery," Enrique added, "to see if we can figure out how and when he got there, and who he was with. Now that we know where you last saw him, we'll pull video and canvass along the routes from Richardson's to the cemetery, as well. Maybe we can find someone who saw him with someone."

"Is there anything I can do to help?"

"Pray," Enrique said.

So that was that.

"Will you let me know what happens?" I asked, getting to my feet. "I'll be here for a while longer. And you know where to find me."

Ricky Fuentes nodded, getting up, too. "Of course, Cassie. I'm sorry this happened. I was looking forward to spending some time with you while you're here."

Out of the corner of my eye, I thought I saw Ty's gaze narrow, but it could have been wishful thinking. Probably was.

"That would be nice," I said demurely. "Thank you for the flowers, by the way."

Enrique managed a smile, although it was more like a grimace. "It seemed the least I could do."

"Maybe you'll figure out what happened to Juan soon. And Stan will be convicted and go to jail for a long time, and then we can go out and celebrate." I smiled back.

"I'd like that," Ricky said, coming around the desk, I guess to escort me out. But then his desk phone rang, and he scowled at it.

"I'll see Cassie out," Ty said. "You take care of that."

He didn't wait for an answer, just put his hand on the small of my back and nudged me out the door. Behind me, I heard Ricky's voice. "Key West PD. Enrique Fuentes speaking."

"Let's go," Ty said, pushing me ahead of him.

I stepped away from his hand. "You don't have to see me out. I can find my way." It wasn't like it was complicated. Straight through the bullpen, straight through the reception area, and straight out the door.

"That's not why," Ty said, sticking to me like glue. Through the bullpen, through reception, and through the door. When

44

we were outside, he turned to me. "You OK?"

"Fine," I said.

"How did your testimony go? That was this morning, right?"

I nodded. "It was hard, but I survived. The prosecutor seemed happy. The public defender reserved the right to recall me to the stand later. Stan smirked at me."

"Bastard," Ty said.

I shrugged. "He's cuffed to his chair. It's not like he can do anything worse than smirk."

Ty shrugged, acknowledging my point.

He was more casually dressed today than yesterday, although not as casually as he'd been last year. Of course, he wasn't pretending to be a college student now. He was here officially as an FBI agent, getting ready to testify at the trial of a man he'd helped apprehend, during a joint investigation he had headed. He was wearing a pair of slacks and a button-down shirt with the sleeves rolled up halfway to his elbows. The color, a sort of oatmeal, set off the bright green of his eyes.

"I saw you and Carmen yesterday," I said, and then wished I hadn't.

He looked at me. I looked away, giving myself a hard mental kick. *Stupid, Cassie.*

"You're the one who wanted to break up," Ty said. When I didn't answer, he added, "Right?"

I blew out a breath. "Right. I wanted to break up."

"So you can't be upset if I get involved with someone else." Like hell I couldn't.

I turned back to him. "It's just... it's Carmen. Didn't you tell me last year that she isn't your type?"

"Maybe I changed my mind," Ty said.

Sure.

"Or maybe the girl who was my type dumped me, and I'm looking for some sympathy."

"I didn't dump you. I just couldn't live with the uncertainty."

The corner of his mouth twitched. "How d'you know I was

talking about you?"

Oh, please. I rolled my eyes. "I'm paying you the compliment of assuming you didn't find someone else the same week we broke up. Or even the same month. I assumed it might take you just a little time to get over me. But if I'm wrong, then I apologize. For all I know, you may have had three or four girlfriends since Thanksgiving."

"No," Ty said.

"Just Carmen?"

He shrugged.

"Well, I'm happy for you." The lie didn't get stuck in my throat. *Amazing.* "And she's Ricky's sister, so she's probably used to the uncertainty of dating someone in law enforcement. She'll be able to handle it a lot better than I did."

"Cassie..." Ty said, but before he could say anything else, the door to the precinct opened and Ricky Fuentes burst through, wild-eyed and disheveled, gun in hand. A couple of other cops followed hard on his heels, and peeled off, one to the left and one to the right, guns out and at the ready.

"Whoa!" I stared after them, mouth open.

Ty snagged me around the waist and pulled me up against him, shielding me with his body. I had no idea from what, and I don't think he did either, but I didn't care. I could feel the heat of his skin all the way down my back, through both our layers of clothes.

He used his other hand to pull his gun. "What's going on?" he asked Enrique, as soon as the latter had reached us.

"Let's get inside." Fuentes put us both in front of him as Ty hustled me up to the door. Once we were inside the building, he—Ty—let go, but continued to push me ahead of him across the bullpen. There was no more quiet buzz of activity; now the bullpen sounded more like a beehive after someone has poked it with a stick. Loud and angry.

Once we were back inside Enrique's office, Enrique said, "That was the bailiff at the Courthouse calling, to ask why Stan hadn't been delivered for the second session of the day."

Ty didn't say anything.

"And why hadn't he?" I asked.

"That's what I had to find out. So I radioed Martoni and Sullivan."

"Who's Martoni and Sullivan?"

"The two officers whose job it was to transport Stan back and forth to the Courthouse," Ty told me, his face as grim as Enrique's. "Are they alive?"

"So far." Although Ricky's voice didn't bode well for what might happen once he got hold of them. "He shot Martoni in the gut and Sullivan in the leg. God only knows how he managed to get hold of a gun. And then he shot the tire out on the car and left."

"Left?" I said. Or croaked, rather. I had to put out a hand and steady myself on the back of the chair I'd been sitting in earlier. "Stan escaped? He's on the loose?"

They exchanged a look. Then Ty took a step closer to me. "We'll protect you, Cassie. I promise. We won't let anything happen to you."

CHAPTER
Five

Here we go again.

"You don't think he's going to come after me, do you?" I asked Ty twenty minutes later, when we were on our way back to the Courthouse.

We were traveling by cab. All the cars, squad and unmarked, that belonged to the Key West PD were on the streets looking for Stan, so there had been nothing for Ricky Fuentes to loan us. And he and Ty both agreed that it wasn't safe for us to walk. Stan had a gun and obviously wasn't afraid to use it. None of us would put it past him to take potshots at us as we walked down the road, endangering not just us but innocent bystanders, and neither of us wanted to put on a bulletproof vest for the walk downtown.

Ty kept looking out the windows in all directions, up and down and all around, keeping an eye out for Stan. He wasn't really paying attention to me, and I was OK with that. I'd rather he keep me alive and in one piece than hang on my every word like he adored me. But this was one question I wanted answered, so when he didn't respond immediately, I kicked his ankle.

"Oww!" He scowled at me. "What?"

"I said, you don't think he's going to come after me, do you?"

"No," Ty said.

"Then why do you keep looking for him?"

He glanced out the window again before he answered. "Because I'd rather look and not see him than assume he isn't there and have him shoot you."

Great. "So you think he will come after me."

"No," Ty said. "If he has any sense at all, he'll get off the island. He'll go as far and as fast as he can. He won't stop to take care of old business."

That'd be nice. But did Stan have that much sense?

"He isn't stupid," Ty said when I brought up this objection, with another look over his shoulder out the window. "He wouldn't have gotten away with what he was doing for as long as he did if he was."

True. Although because he did get away with it for so long, he might just consider getting caught a spectacular stroke of bad luck, one that wouldn't have happened if not for me. So he might sincerely think that he was smart enough to stay in Key West and kill me, without anyone being able to catch him.

"I'll make sure nothing happens to you, Cassie," Ty said, reaching for my hand. His eyes were deep and green and terribly sincere, and his voice was lovely and warm. And then he ruined it by adding, "It's my job. I'm good at it."

I twitched my hand out of his. "I'm sure you are. Keep watching the street, please."

His mouth curved, but he did as I said. After a minute he picked up the conversation again. "Enrique will catch up to him soon. It isn't easy to leave a place like Key West. There's only one road out of town, and that road is two lanes wide. By now, Enrique will have roadblocks as far away as Marathon and Key Largo. Stan doesn't have a hope of getting to the mainland."

I twisted my head to look out the window. There was no sign of Stan. "Wouldn't it be easier to grab a boat? There's a lot of water around here. And a lot of islands." Many of them uninhabited but for snakes, lizards, and other critters. Plenty of places to hide for a while. "Not to mention a lot of boats."

"Harder to patrol the sea," Ty admitted, "although the Coast Guard's out. We'll catch him."

I hoped they would, because I knew I wouldn't draw an easy breath again until they did.

Back at the Courthouse, it looked like a siege was taking place. The front doors were locked and barred, both sets of them: the inner doors with the louvers, and the outer doors—solid wood—that fit in front of them. The back door was guarded by Don the security guard. He looked us both up and down several times before consenting to opening the door for us.

"Thank you, Don," I said graciously.

Ty grunted something, and I don't think it was a thank you. "Who's still here?"

"Everyone," Don said. And amended it to, "The audience and reporters left. This will be headline news tomorrow morning. But Judge Andrews and the bailiff are both in chambers, while Mr. Berryman and Mr. DeWitt are hanging out in the courtroom."

"What about Paula and her mother?" I asked.

"Also there. Detective Fuentes said to keep everyone important here until he catches the prisoner."

Who wasn't technically a prisoner anymore. And while I appreciated—and admired—Enrique's confidence that getting Stan back behind bars would be a simple task, I wasn't sure I agreed with him. I had a feeling I'd be sleeping with one eye open for the next few nights.

"I'd like to see Paula and Mrs. Carlson," I told Ty, who nodded.

"I'll be right there." He turned back to Don.

Paula and her mother were pale, clutching one another on the front row. Mr. DeWitt was still at the prosecution table and Mr. Berryman at the defense table. Every one of them turned when I stepped across the threshold.

"Oh," Mr. Berryman said after a moment. "We thought it might be news."

"Sorry. I don't think I know any more than you do." I made my way toward them and scooted in next to Paula and Mrs. Carlson. "I was still at the police station when Detective Fuentes got the news. It took us a while to get here."

"Us?" Berryman repeated, ears pricking.

I glanced at Mr. DeWitt, who gave me no direction whatsoever. I turned back to Berryman. "Agent Connor and I traveled together. He was at the police station, too. So he volunteered to escort me back here while Detective Fuentes and all the police officers in Key West went out to look for your client."

Berryman muttered something, but subsided.

"Ty said they have roadblocks set up on US-1 as far away as Marathon and Key Largo," I added. "They're checking the buses leaving town, as well. And the Coast Guard is patrolling, in case he decides to try to escape by water. They seem confident he won't get far."

Nobody said anything, but their expressions said plenty. Guess I wasn't the only one who had doubts. Stan was a native. He might have friends who'd help him, and he certainly knew more about the Keys than those of us who were only visiting.

After a moment, Berryman and Mr. DeWitt turned to one another and began a low-voiced conversation. I tried to listen with one ear while paying attention to Paula with the other, but she was closer, and they were speaking very softly, so I only caught a word now and then.

From them, not from Paula. I heard everything she said, loud and clear.

"I'm afraid, Cassie."

I nodded. "I know. Me too."

She dropped her voice to a whisper. "What if they don't catch him? What if he comes after us?"

I wasn't sure whether that "us" meant her and me, or her and her mother, but I'm not sure it mattered. "You should probably go home," I said. "I know you wanted to meet Mackenzie, but with Stan on the loose, if they don't catch him today, you'll probably feel better back in Wisconsin. He won't go there."

"We're leaving tomorrow," Mrs. Carlson said firmly. Paula glanced at her, but didn't speak. Nonetheless, her mother added, "Don't even try to talk me out of it. If that man's walking around free—and with a gun!—we don't want to be in the same state he is, let alone the same small island."

Paula nodded. "What about you, Cassie? Are you going back to Chicago?"

I hesitated. It was tempting. Chicago sounded safe, just as safe as Wisconsin. It was far away from Key West, and the chances of Stan going there, or getting there without being caught, were slim. Braxton sounded even safer, although if I was wrong and Stan did manage to travel, I wasn't about to lead him to my mom and dad. And anyway, if Ty was here and going after Stan, I had to stick around to make sure Ty was safe. "Not right now. I don't have a ticket out for a week and a half anyway."

"You can change your ticket," Mrs. Carlson pointed out.

I could. But that meant I'd miss seeing Quinn and Mackenzie next week, because I couldn't afford to go back to Chicago and then come back to Key West a second time in a week. "I think I'll wait a day or two before I decide. See if they catch him."

Paula bit her lip. "You'll be careful, won't you, Cassie?"

"Of course I will," I said. "And Agent Connor and the police will protect me. I'll be fine."

I wasn't a hundred percent sure of that myself, of course, but I didn't want to worry Paula any more. And I especially didn't want to do anything to make her think she had to stay in Key West out of solidarity. I already felt guilty enough about the trouble I'd gotten her into last time we were both here. I certainly didn't want to give Stan another shot at her.

"Where are you staying?" I asked Mrs. Carlson.

She gave me the name of a bed and breakfast in the historic district.

"If you don't mind a piece of advice, maybe it would be a good idea to spend tonight in a hotel. One of the new ones, that have good security and a doorman. Maybe even something right next to the airport. You might be safer there."

"Is that what you're going to do, Cassie?" Paula asked, while her mother thought about my suggestion.

I would if I could afford it. But my budget didn't stretch to anything fancier that Richardson's Motel.

I was saved from answering when the door to the hallway opened and Ty came in.

Berryman was first to speak again. "Any news?"

"I came here with Cassie," Ty said. "I've been outside talking to the security guard. I'm sure you know as much as I do."

He closed the door behind him and came toward us. Berryman turned back to Mr. DeWitt and picked up their conversation.

I waited for Ty to sit down next to me. "Did he have anything interesting to say?"

Ty shook his head. "Nothing happened here. It all took place somewhere else. Don didn't hear about it until Enrique told him to shut down the Courthouse and keep everyone inside."

"How long do we have to stay here?"

He quirked a brow at me. "Somewhere else you'd rather be?"

"I'd rather be at my place in Chicago," I said, "a safe distance from Stan. But barring that, I wouldn't mind stopping by the hospital to see Juan."

Ty nodded. He looked perfectly calm now, but I swear something had shifted in his eyes for a second when I'd mentioned my place in Chicago. For six months or so, it had been *our* place in Chicago. I guess he remembered. And no doubt he'd rather be there than here, too.

"Who's Juan?" Paula wanted to know, surreptitiously watching Ty. He's twenty-six by now, but looks at least three or four years younger, so she probably didn't realize he was too old for her.

She probably didn't realize I had a prior claim, either. On the stand, I had made it very clear that Ty and I were not involved, nor had we been involved during Spring Break last year. And nobody had asked me about the time in-between.

Then again, I'd had him and had dropped him, so maybe I had no right to object to anyone else zooming in and picking him up, whether that someone was Paula or Carmen.

Paula's mother must have noticed the byplay, however, because she made quick work of putting Ty in his proper place in the chain of command. "Agent Connor—"

She shot a sideways glance at Paula, to make sure her daughter recognized that this was an FBI agent she was looking at, a law enforcement professional well out of her league.

"Yes, Mrs. Carlson?" Ty said politely.

"We don't know much about what happened. We've been here." She gestured around the practically empty courtroom, free of anyone who might know anything about what had gone on somewhere else. "Would you mind explaining?"

"Not at all," Ty said, and did. Mrs. Carlson clapped a hand over her mouth when he got to the part about the wounded cops, and Paula looked sick.

"That's barbaric," Mrs. Carlson said from behind her hand. "Will they be all right?"

Ty hesitated. "Sullivan will be fine. He got shot in the leg. In the fleshy part of the calf. An inch or two to either side, and the bullet would have missed him altogether. He'll have to recuperate for a few weeks and take it easy afterwards, but chances are he'll be back on duty in a month. Martoni..." He hesitated.

"He'll be all right, won't he?" I'd never even met the injured Martoni, but poor Ricky Fuentes would never get over it if his assigning Martoni to guard Stan had resulted in Martoni's death.

"He lost a lot of blood," Ty said reluctantly. "He's lucky he was found as quickly as he was. But the bullet missed anything vital. And the paramedics started transfusions immediately. Last I heard, they thought he'd pull through."

"Can we stop and see him, when we go to the hospital to see Juan?"

"Sure," Ty said. "We have to stay here until they find Stan, though, Cassie."

Or until they admitted defeat and told us it would take longer than they thought, more likely. But I didn't say that.

CHAPTER
Six

The call came at six-thirty. By then we had gotten tired of sitting in the courtroom and had adjourned to the anteroom, where at least there was a TV we could watch. The prosecutor and public defender had gone to join Judge Andrews and his bailiff in the judge's chambers, as chummy as you please. When they didn't come back, I assumed there was a TV there, too.

Mrs. Carlson, Paula, Ty, and I were watching a sitcom that had aired originally before most of us were born. The local news was all about Stan escaping by shooting two police officers, and how he was considered armed and extremely dangerous. If spotted, do not approach; call the police tip line immediately.

There was no information beyond that rather sensational tidbit—Mrs. Carlson and Paula turned paler and paler every time the news anchor said the same thing—and none of us wanted to watch a rerun of Law & Order: SVU, since it cut a little too close to the bone for several of us. So we were chuckling along with the Full House gang.

At six-thirty, Ty's phone rang. We all froze as we watched him dig the phone out of his pocket and put it to his ear. "Connor."

Business call. If it had been personal, he would have said something else. His name or "Yo, dawg," just to be funny.

The phone quacked for a few seconds, then a few seconds more. "Got it," Ty said. "Thanks."

He turned the phone off and dropped it back in his pocket before facing us. "We can go."

"They caught him?" Mrs. Carlson looked surprised but elated. And looked like someone being told there is no Santa Claus when Ty shook his head.

"No. But they don't want to keep us here any longer. Sunset's in an hour. They want us safely inside by dark. There'll be two cars outside the back door in five minutes to transport us to where we're going."

He got up. "Excuse me. I have to go tell the judge and attorneys."

He headed out, leaving us there.

"This is scary," Paula said after a moment. Her mother reached for her hand, and it was hard to say who was comforting whom.

"They'll catch him," I told them both. "It's an island, so it's easy to monitor who comes and goes. There's only one road out of here. If he tries to leave Key West, he'll be caught. And it's a small island, so sooner or later someone will notice him. It's just a matter of time."

Paula nodded, but swallowed. "I want to go home."

"Tomorrow," her mother said.

Paula tried a laugh, but it wasn't very convincing. "I don't even care about meeting Mackenzie Forbes anymore."

"You can always meet Mackenzie Forbes," I told her. "Just come visit me in Chicago, and I'll introduce you."

Paula nodded.

I added, "Besides, after this, she may not even be coming

here. They may be shutting down Key West. With last year's rapist on the loose, they're not going to want to add a whole lot of new potential victims to the mix. Everyone who was coming for Spring Break may have to go somewhere else. Or wait until after he gets caught, if it takes that long."

Mrs. Carlson nodded agreement. "We'll get you to Chicago sometime, honey, if you want to meet Mackenzie Forbes. Cassie will introduce you. But I've had enough of Key West for now. Tomorrow we're going home."

"Yes, Mama," Paula said. They got up and headed for the back door, the better to wait for the car that would be arriving. I turned off the TV and followed.

Ty had herded Judge Andrews, the bailiff, the court reporter—whom I had forgotten until now—Berryman the public defender and DeWitt the prosecutor, into the hallway by the back door. Without his severe black robes, the judge looked like a normal, reasonably friendly old guy. He nodded to us as he headed out the door to the first car. "Have a good evening, all. Stay safe."

He took the bailiff, the court reporter, and Berryman the public defender with him, leaving Don the security guard and Mr. DeWitt for us. The lawyer got into the second car with Paula and her mom, I guess for a last minute chat before they left tomorrow. "Cassie?" Mr. DeWitt turned to me.

"I've got her," Ty said, which sounded promising.

"What are we doing?" I asked him as the second car drove off without us. Not that there was room for two more inside, although I suppose I could have sat on his lap for a while.

Or not.

"Enrique's on his way. He's going to the hospital, so I hitched us a ride."

"Oh." That was nice of him to think of. "Thank you."

He shrugged. "I wouldn't mind seeing Juan. And I want to be there for the interviews with Sullivan and Martoni."

Of course. Duty first. It wasn't that he'd tried to make me happy at all. Just that since he and Enrique were going to the hospital anyway, I might as well come along.

Ricky Fuentes pulled up a few silent minutes later, and Don made sure the Courthouse door latched and locked behind us. He stood by, gun drawn, while we crossed the few feet of open ground and crawled into Enrique's car; me in the back and Ty up front with Enrique. And then we waited until Don had crossed the parking lot and was safely inside his own car before both cars pulled out of the lot and headed in different directions.

"News?" Ty enquired as soon as we were moving.

"The road blocks are in place," Ricky said. "The Coast Guard is patrolling. The tip line is going crazy with calls. Stan has been spotted everywhere from the Key West Cemetery to Sloppy Joe's Bar to walking down Duval in broad daylight. One woman swore she'd seen him playing with the cats at the Hemingway House, and one man said he'd seen him set out from the Southernmost Point to swim to Cuba."

That last one did seem rather unlikely. It's only ninety miles between Key West and Cuba, considerably less than between Key West and mainland Florida, at least along US-1. And I could imagine Stan wanting to get to Cuba if he thought it would keep him from going back to prison. But I doubted he'd swim. Much easier and safer to borrow a boat.

"What are you doing about the tips?" I wanted to know, leaning forward between the seats.

Ricky glanced at me in the rearview mirror. "We can't follow them all. There are too many tips and too few of us, especially with two of my officers in the hospital and two more playing chauffeur. I had to pull the guard off Juan just to do what I'm doing."

"What's the point of having a tip line if you don't follow up on the tips?"

There was a grinding sound. Perhaps from the car, but more likely from Enrique gritting his teeth. "We're following up. We just have to choose to follow the tips that seem the most promising. I don't think he's swimming to Cuba, but we alerted the Coast Guard just in case. The bartender at Sloppy Joe's knows Stan by sight, and said he hadn't been in. I didn't bother to follow up with the Hemingway House, and I don't think he'd be stupid enough to walk down Duval in broad daylight."

Probably not. "Is anyone checking Sunset Key and Wisteria Island and all the other little islands up near Jewfish Basin? He could lie in wait up there for a long, long time without anyone finding him."

"The Coast Guard is patrolling," Enrique said. It was starting to sound like a refrain.

He was also starting to sound frustrated, so I sat back and let them talk without imposing my opinions on them. They were the professionals, and they didn't need me to tell them their jobs. It was just that I was nervous, and being involved, however peripherally, made me feel better.

For some reason I had assumed we'd end up at the same hospital I'd gone to last year, after Stan drugged me. We didn't. Instead we crossed the bridge from Key West to Stock Island, and headed up past the Botanical Gardens to the Lower Keys Medical Center. Which made sense once I thought about it, since the tiny hospital from last year was attached to a women's medical clinic, and naturally Juan and the two wounded officers wouldn't be going there.

We stopped by Juan's room first. As Enrique had said, there was no longer an officer on the door, but Carmen was sitting next to the bed flipping the pages of a fashion magazine. When we walked in, she dropped it to her lap. "Finally!"

And then she saw me. "Cassie!"

"Carmen." I gave her a hug, because I couldn't get out of it. And because I'd liked her last year, after I realized she didn't have designs on Ty. I didn't like her so much this year, but since I didn't want to hurt her feelings—and since I didn't want Ty to think I still cared—I did my best to hide it. "How are you? How's Juan?"

He looked awful. The arm where the IV was attached was

discolored from bruises, limp and flaccid, the golden skin more a sickly yellow under the florescent lighting. His face was jaundiced, too; the lips dry, and spiky eyelashes lay quiet in sunken eye sockets. He had bandages wrapped around his head, with tufts of black curls peeking out here and there.

"I'm so sorry," I told Carmen, my eyes tearing up.

"It's not your fault." She put an arm around my shoulders. She's a couple inches taller than I am, and the heels added another few inches. "It's the fault of whoever hurt him. You had no idea it would happen."

No, but I still felt bad. Maybe if I hadn't accepted his offer to walk me home, if I'd just left him at Captain Crow's and gone home on my own, he wouldn't have met whoever hurt him.

"Any news?" Carmen asked Enrique, who shook his head, grimly.

"We're on our way to see Sullivan and Martoni. Maybe one of them has something helpful to contribute. If nothing else, I'd like to know who was careless enough to let Stan get the drop on him."

"Sullivan," Carmen said.

Enrique arched a brow, and she added, "I went to school with him, too. He tolerated Stan a bit better than some of the rest of us."

"Pretty sure the gun was Martoni's," Enrique said. "That's why Stan got him point blank in the stomach and only winged Sullivan in the calf."

Carmen shrugged. Her breasts moved. I tried not to be jealous, but couldn't quite manage.

When I glanced at Ty, he was watching me. The curve of his mouth was amused. I looked away.

"He still under?" Enrique asked, looking at Juan. Juan's breathing was so shallow his chest under the blankets hardly rose and fell at all.

Carmen nodded. "Until tomorrow. They'll try to bring him around then. If there's no change."

"I'll try to be here. But with what's going on, I'm not sure I can be."

"The rest of us will come," Carmen said. "*Mamá* understands that it's your job to catch Stan and the people who did this to Juan. We all want you to do that."

Enrique nodded. "If I can be here, I will. If not, let me know how it goes."

"Of course, '*mano*.'" She reached up and gave him a hug. "Are you going to see your cops now?"

He nodded. "You want a ride home when we're done?"

"Yes, please," Carmen said. "I'll stay here till then." She sat back in the chair by the bed and picked up the magazine.

Enrique nodded to the door, and Ty followed him out in the hallway. At the last moment, he turned. "Cassie? You coming?"

"Yessir." I scurried down the hall after them.

We stopped by Martoni's room first. He was right around the corner from Juan, being the more severely injured. And like Juan, he was in no position to give anyone his side of the story. He wasn't in an induced coma, so he was awake—more or less—but not really aware. The morphine drip going into his arm probably had a lot to do with it. When Enrique walked through the door, he managed a goofy smile and a twitch of the unencumbered hand. I assumed it was supposed to be a wave, but it really was just a twitch. And although he opened his mouth, nothing came out.

Enrique stopped by the bedside, and as Ty and I sidled up next to him—or I sidled; Ty walked, like he had every right to be there—I realized I'd met Martoni before. Last year, Enrique had sent a cop to drive me from the hotel to the women's clinic. He'd had strict instructions not to talk to me, so we hadn't exchanged more than the obligatory, "Thanks for the ride, Officer," and "My pleasure, miss," when he dropped me off, but it was definitely him.

He probably didn't recognize me, though, and now wasn't

the time to remind him.

"You OK, man?" Enrique wanted to know.

Martoni didn't answer, but I saw the movement as his eyes slid toward the IV, and the slight upward curl of his lips. I guess the medicine was helping, and probably making him feel nicely floaty, too.

"Any pain?" Ricky asked.

Seemingly not, because Martoni managed a very slight right to left movement of his head on the pillow, with another glance at the IV.

"I'll check back with you tomorrow. You should try to get as much rest as you can. I'm gonna want your report as soon as possible."

Martoni looked distressed. His eyebrows drew together. He made an attempt to pluck at Ricky's sleeve and opened his mouth. Enrique leaned closer. "What?"

"Sully…"

"He's all right," Ricky said. "Better than you. Took a bullet in the calf, but should be outta here in a day or so. You'll have to stay a little longer."

Martoni looked frustrated. He opened his mouth again.

"What?"

"Stan…"

It was just as much lip-reading as hearing, because he hardly made any noise at all.

"Still on the loose," Ricky said. "But we'll get him. Everyone's looking, and the tip line is getting hundreds of calls."

That didn't seem to be what Martoni wanted to hear, because he still looked frustrated. But he also looked tired, and sank back into the pillows without trying to communicate any more. He was white around the lips from the exertion.

"I'll be back tomorrow," Ricky told him again. "Get some rest."

We filed out, quietly. Behind us, Martoni closed his eyes.

"That's the same guy you sent to drive me to the clinic last year," I told Enrique when we were outside in the hallway.

He nodded, frustration evident on his face. "One of our best officers. Hopefully this isn't the end of his career."

"D'you think he helped Laszlo escape?" Ty asked.

Enrique turned to him, and for a moment he seemed speechless. "No!" he said eventually.

Ty shrugged. "It was either deliberate or careless. Your choice."

Enrique was silent for another moment. And then another. "Hard to believe it was either. He's not usually careless, and I've seen no signs he sympathized with Stan. They weren't close. Besides, he almost died."

"Keyword," Ty said, "almost. Besides, if they planned it together, Laszlo had a very good reason for wanting Martoni dead. He might know where Laszlo is."

Enrique shook his head. "I bet he doesn't. I'd stake my reputation on it."

"Looks like you already are," Ty said.

Enrique grimaced. "Let's see if Sullivan is awake. We're likely to get more out of him."

We set off again.

Sullivan was on a different floor, out of the ICU. He was sitting in bed with a blanket over his lap and a bandaged leg sticking out, surfing TV channels. When we walked in, he put the remote down. "Detective Fuentes."

He looked apprehensive. Maybe he was afraid Enrique was going to yell at him.

"Officer Sullivan." Enrique nodded. "How are you feeling?"

Sullivan shook his head. He was a smallish guy, with dark hair and a heavy five-o'clock-shadow. "Not so good, Detective. Cody..."

"We've seen Martoni," Enrique said.

"Is he gonna be OK?" Sullivan tried to straighten, and winced.

"He's hanging in. Heavily sedated. Wasn't able to talk."

Sullivan's face relaxed again. I guess he'd gotten into a position he liked.

"You're gonna have to tell us what happened," Enrique said.

Sullivan's face tightened again. Maybe it wasn't the physical pain so much as the anticipation that bothered him. "I don't know what happened, Detective."

"You were there, weren't you?"

"Sure," Sullivan said, "but it all happened so fast..."

Enrique didn't say anything, just waited, and after a few moments, Sullivan continued. "We were on our way back to the Courthouse after lunch. We were running late to begin with, because Stan spent a lotta time in the head before we left. Suddenly he began making these noises in the back of the car like he was dying. We tried asking him what was wrong, but he just groaned. So we thought maybe he'd eaten something, you know, that didn't agree with him? Like, he was gonna hurl right there in the car?"

Enrique nodded.

"I pulled over, and Cody got out to check on him. Next thing, I hear a shot, and Cody goes down. Stan's out of the car and running. I try to follow, but he shoots at me, too. And Cody's down and I don't know whether he's dead or alive. So I let Stan go and get back to Cody and try to do what I can for him, and then the radio goes off wondering why I'm not at the Courthouse with Stan—"

He must have run out of words and breath at the same time.

"And you have no idea what happened."

Sullivan shook his head. "No, sir. One second he was sitting there groaning, the next he was out of the car and running. Or at least it felt almost that fast."

We were all silent for a moment.

"Did you or did Officer Martoni have the keys to the handcuffs?" Ty wanted to know.

Sullivan's face went blank for a second, and Ty continued, "Is it possible your partner opened the prisoner's cuffs when he leaned into the backseat?"

Sullivan blinked. "We each have keys," he said.

Enrique nodded. "You know how it is, Agent Connor. You can't always hunt down the arresting officer when you need a set of handcuffs taken off. The keys are universal. All our handcuffs are Smith & Wesson, and all our keys open all our handcuffs."

Ty didn't look surprised. The FBI probably operated the same way. Although I'd never seen Ty carry handcuffs. In undercover work, I guess you don't.

"So you think your partner might have removed Laszlo's handcuffs?"

"I wouldn't wanna say..." Sullivan demurred, which was a lot like saying, really.

"Try this. Which one of you put the cuffs on the prisoner? One of you, or someone at the prison?"

"Someone at the prison," Sullivan said promptly. "But I checked'em when we picked him up."

"And they were secure?"

"Yeah. Sure." He shifted his attention to Enrique. "Any word on Stan, Detective?"

"He's still out there," Fuentes said. "But everyone's looking for him, and the tip line's getting calls every minute. We'll get him."

He took a step toward the door. "We'll let you get some rest, Sully. You'll be back on duty before you know it. We need every hand on deck right now."

Sullivan nodded, looking a bit more cheerful. Enrique gestured Ty and me toward the door. Just before we all ducked out, Sullivan asked, a bit tentatively, "Detective? How's your brother doing?"

Enrique hesitated. I guess maybe he wasn't sure how much to tell someone who was both a subordinate and on the hot seat at the moment. Or maybe he just didn't know what to say. "Not so good, Sully," he said eventually. "They're gonna try to wake him up tomorrow. If they can."

Sullivan turned a shade paler. "I'm sorry, Detective," he

managed, his voice half choked.

Enrique nodded, he face grim. I guess a "Thank you," was beyond him under the circumstances. And then we were out the door and in the hallway once again.

CHAPTER
Seven

We picked up Carmen in Juan's room—he was still unconscious and she was still flipping through Marie Claire—and headed out. It was a quick drive; just a few minutes to the Fuentes family home.

Carmen left the car first. When nobody else moved, she looked back over her shoulder. "Isn't anybody else coming in?"

"I have to go back to work," Enrique said. "I'm gonna be working 24/7 for a while."

Carmen put her hands on her hips. "*Mamá* won't like that."

"*Mamá* will have to deal," Enrique said. "Between Stan escaping and what happened to Juan, my hands are full."

Carmen shrugged. She moved her attention to Ty.

"I'm sticking with Cassie," he told her. "In case Stan shows up. She can't be left alone."

Sheesh, he sounded like he'd rather have a root canal.

Carmen flipped her masses of hair over her shoulder. "Cassie can come, too."

It wasn't the most gracious invitation I've ever heard, but at least she hadn't suggested I could go back to the police station with Ricky while she kept Ty for the evening.

"Some other time," Ty said. "Enjoy your family. Stay safe. We'll see you tomorrow."

Carmen pouted, but went. We waited until the door had closed behind her, and then Enrique put the car in gear. "Richardson's?"

"Please," I said.

He glanced at me in the rearview, but didn't say anything. Ty's cheek curved, like he was smiling, but since he was in the front seat and I was in the back, I couldn't be sure.

The two of them got busy talking procedure, whether the trial would be postponed until Stan reappeared or whether he could be convicted *in absentia*. I didn't get involved, although I have to say that while convicting and sentencing Stan would go a long way toward making me feel better, I wouldn't be happy unless he actually had to serve whatever sentence he got. Knowing he was out there, walking around like a free man— if one who had to keep looking over his shoulder—wasn't enough to satisfy me. Especially because, at the moment, I was the one looking over my shoulder in case he came gunning for me.

But if he planned to, he had something else to do at the moment. The trip to Richardson's Motel was uneventful. The sidewalks were busy, but I saw no sign of Stan. And when we got there, the motel looked just as it had when Juan walked me home... was it just yesterday?

The office was closed, a group of people were hanging out by the pool—probably the same group as yesterday—and the light was on above my door, shining on the pot of red flowers.

"Hang on," Ty told me when I reached for the door handle.

"I'm capable of walking to the door on my own. It's just over there." I pointed to it. "You can sit here and watch me."

It was Enrique's turn to smile. He didn't speak, though. Ty took care of that.

"That won't do any good if he's hiding inside."

"There's nowhere to hide," I told him, just as I'd told Juan yesterday. "Platform bed, no closet, and a tiny shower. You should know that. You stayed here last year."

"I'm staying here this year, too."

He grinned at my stupefied expression, and then opened his own door. "Cover us," he told Enrique. I rolled my eyes, but only until Enrique slipped out of the car, pulled his gun, and braced his arms on the roof of the car. Then it started to feel a little too real.

"Come on out, Cassie."

Sure. I opened the door and slithered out.

"Stay low," Enrique warned, peering into the darkness on the other side of the street.

Yeah, yeah.

Then Ty was there, and gathered me in front of him. "Room 107," he said into my ear.

"Why can't we go—?" –*to my room?*

"There's a gun in mine. Besides, he won't look for you there."

Sure he would, if he had any sense. Although he'd probably come to my room first, so maybe it would be better if I were somewhere else.

Ty nudged me into motion toward his end of the wing. Behind us, Enrique kept an eye out for movement across the street. It was nice of him, although to be honest, if Stan suddenly showed up and shot at us, there wouldn't be anything Enrique could do about deflecting the bullet. He could just try to shoot Stan, and hope that Stan hadn't killed one of us.

But nothing happened. We made it to the door safely. Ty kept me in front of him while he fumbled out his key—with a turquoise tag, like mine—and inserted it in the lock. He pushed the door open and snaked a hand around the jamb for the light. Then he pushed me in ahead of him, and slammed the door behind us.

Outside, Enrique holstered the gun and slid back into the car. Ty did a quick circuit of the room—nobody was hiding behind the shower curtain or the bathroom door—before cracking the door and waving Enrique off. The car pulled away and the rear lights disappeared down the street.

I looked around. Ty's room looked just like mine. Same non-descript tile floor, same off-white walls, same nubby blanket on the bed. The picture of a beach above the bed was different, but it was still a picture of a beach.

"Homey," I said.

He grinned. "Looks like yours, does it?"

"Everything but the picture. And the gun." He'd taken it out of a small box that had been in a bureau drawer. "I didn't realize you carried one."

"When I'm undercover I can't. Unless my cover is someone who'd carry a gun. But most of them aren't. Not when you're trying to pass for eighteen." He was handling it knowledgeably, anyway. Opening it to put in bullets, peering down the barrel, or whatever it is one does with a gun.

"You know how to use it, I assume?" I asked.

He glanced at me, and then smiled. "Of course. The bureau makes sure I can hit what I aim at, and that I'm not a menace to society. Every so often I have to prove it."

Good to know. "I don't remember you having one in Chicago."

"I didn't bring it with me when I came to see you," Ty said. "And we didn't live together. Officially."

No, we hadn't. Although he'd certainly spent enough time at my place. Albeit without the gun.

"You know, Cassie..." He wasn't looking at me, but was still fiddling with the weapon, "I didn't join the FBI to do undercover work."

"You didn't?"

He shook his head. "I told you last year, I studied psychology in college. I wanted to be a profiler. But when I joined, somebody looked at me and thought that since I look the way I do..."

"Young."

He nodded. "They could use me to go undercover in gangs and colleges. I'm not going to be doing this forever. Another couple years, and I'll be too old to pass for eighteen, or even twenty-two."

Sure. But why tell me so?

"What about Carmen?" I asked.

"What about her?"

"I was looking at the two of you yesterday. You were so busy watching her testify, you didn't even see me come in. And later, at Captain Crow's..."

He shook his head. "I saw you, Cassie. But you dumped me, remember?"

"It wasn't a dump," I said.

"We broke up. You can't take it personally if I get involved with someone else."

I knew that. Although it didn't stop me.

I turned from him to the door. "Now that you have your gun, can you walk me to my room?"

"You're not going to your room," Ty said.

"What do you mean? Of course I'm going to my room!" I certainly couldn't stay with him in his.

"Pretend this is your room."

I stared at him, and he added, "You said it looks the same. It shouldn't be too much of a stretch."

"I'm not spending the night with you!"

The corner of his mouth quirked. "Bet I could change your mind."

No bet. I was sure he could, too. With hardly any effort at all. But that didn't mean I wanted him to.

Much.

"If you wanted sex, you should have gone inside with Carmen."

I half expected him to make some sort of joke about sex and Carmen's parents' house. He didn't. "I'm not sleeping with Carmen," he said instead.

Could have fooled me.

I didn't say it, although my face must have said something, because he added, "You think Enrique would be this nice to me if I was banging his sister?"

Well... maybe not.

"It's none of my business," I said. "I dumped you, remember?"

"I thought you said it wasn't a dump."

Yeah, yeah. "I want to go to my room. I'm hungry. We didn't have dinner and there are granola bars there."

"I'll order a pizza," Ty said, and reached for his phone. "Green pepper and black olive?"

I sat down on the bed, since there wasn't anything else I could do, and nowhere else I could sit. "Yeah." Annoying, how well he knew me.

The room did have a small TV, but Ty refused to let me turn it on. "I might not hear somebody outside if there's noise in here," he explained.

"The pizza guy will knock."

"I'm not worried about the pizza guy. I'm worried about someone taking a shot at you through the window. That's why we have to keep the lights off, too." He walked over to the door and plunged the room into darkness. "With the lights on, you're lit up like a silhouette in a shooting gallery."

I huffed but put the remote down. "So what are we supposed to do while we wait for the pizza?" And how were we supposed to eat it, if we couldn't see?

"Your eyes will adjust to the dark," Ty said, and came to sit next to me on the bed. (It was the only place to sit in the room. Unless he wanted to put himself squarely in front of the window, and I guess he didn't.) "And we could always make out while we wait."

"In your dreams," I said.

I couldn't see him smile, but I could hear it in his voice. "The sex was good, wasn't it?"

Yes, it was. Or had been. However...

"Not like I'd know the difference, is it? I was a virgin before you."

There was a beat. Then his voice came again. "How about after me?"

Dammit. I sighed. "Nobody after you, either."

He didn't say anything to that. And it probably wasn't because he was overwhelmed by the news. So we just sat in silence for a few minutes.

As he'd promised, my eyes did adjust to the dark. Fairly soon I could see not just his outline, but the paler oval that was his face, and the glint of his eyes and teeth when he smiled. "How about we talk, then? We got pretty good at that too, as I recall."

We had, actually. A year ago, it wasn't the sex I'd fallen in love with—because we hadn't had any. He'd barely kissed me. No, I'd fallen in love with his personality. We'd talked. A lot.

"We're already talking," I pointed out.

"I don't wanna talk about us anymore."

That didn't sound encouraging. But since I didn't want him to think I wanted there to be an 'us' again, I didn't say so. "What do you want to talk about?"

"The case," Ty said.

"Juan's case?" Stan's case was closed, wasn't it? Unless he started raping women again, but surely he wouldn't be that stupid. His face was plastered all over the news. The safest thing he could do was lie low, and then get himself out of Key West at the first opportunity.

"All of it," Ty said. He gestured, indicating something big and round. It happened to be with the hand that had the gun in it. The light from the pool area reflected off the barrel.

"Would you mind putting that down?" I asked, scooting away. "I'm glad you have it, but when you're waving it around like that, you're making me nervous."

"Sorry." He put it on the bed next to his hip.

I eyed it. Not that I could see it in the dark, but I looked at the patch of darkness where I assumed it was. "Is that safe?

What if it goes off accidentally? You could shoot yourself in... you know."

"The knee?" He shook his head. "It isn't gonna go off accidentally. Glocks are made without safeties, so it takes more effort to fire one. And I don't want to put it somewhere I can't reach it in a hurry."

Fine. But he could forget about us getting busy on this bed as long as the gun was there.

Then again, I'd already announced we weren't going to get busy on the bed, so he probably wasn't expecting us to.

"So about the case," I said.

"Yeah. What did you think of the trip to the hospital?"

What was there to say about a trip to the hospital to see one guy who'd been beaten up and two others who'd been shot? "Um... horrible?"

"Beyond that," Ty said.

"Well..." I wracked my brain to come up with something halfway intelligent. "Juan looked bad. But I guess he must be getting better if they're thinking of waking him up tomorrow."

Ty nodded.

"It's nice of Carmen to sit with him."

"She's his sister," Ty said. "What else would she do?"

I guess... nothing? I'm an only child, so I don't know much about it.

"I didn't realize Martoni was the same guy who drove us to the clinic last year. I liked him. He didn't say anything, but he seemed friendly."

Ty nodded.

"And Ricky said some very nice things about him. He must be a good police officer. And now he might never be the same. It's horrible."

My voice wobbled a little. It was all getting to be too much. Juan and Martoni and Sullivan in the hospital, and Stan on the loose with a gun in his hand. If he'd shot both Martoni and Sullivan, guys he'd worked with, what might he do to me? Or to Ty, if he got a chance at him?

Ty reached out and took my hand. "We'll get him, Cassie. Someone will see him and call in a tip, and he'll be back in prison. And this time, we'll tack a few counts of attempted murder and assault on a police officer to the charges, as well. He won't see daylight again."

"That's only if he shows up somewhere he can be caught. He might have left Key West and sailed to Cuba, and they'll never send him back."

"I don't care where he went," Ty said. "I'll go there and bring him back. If I have to sneak into Havana and knock him over the head and swim back to Key West dragging him behind me, I'll do it. I promise."

I sniffed. "Thank you."

He nodded. My eyes had gotten adjusted enough to the light by now that I could see him pretty clearly. He was looking at me. Looking at my mouth, unless I was mistaken.

I held my breath as he leaned in.

Yep, definitely looking at my mouth.

My own eyes drifted shut as he came closer.

And just as he was about to kiss me—with no protest on my part—there was a knock on the door.

CHAPTER

Ty jerked back. "Shit!"

He sounded out of breath, although our lips hadn't actually had a chance to connect.

Even so, I was a bit breathless myself. Enough that when he grabbed the gun and moved to the window, I wasn't able to tell him to be careful.

He tilted the curtain about an inch to the side and peered out through the crack.

The knock came again. "Delivery!"

It didn't sound like Stan's voice. And it must not have been Stan, because Ty went to the door and opened it. "Thanks, man. How much do I owe you?" He reached for the pizza box and a plastic bag that held the bottle of Sprite we'd ordered.

The delivery guy took a nervous step back. "I don't want any trouble, man. Just take the pizza. I'll—" He gestured over his shoulder.

"Don't be stupid." Ty stuffed the gun into his waistband at the middle of his back and dug some bills out of his pocket. He handed them over without looking at them. "Here. Did you happen to see anyone hanging around outside?"

The guy tucked the money away without looking at it, too. His hand was shaking. "Just the people by the pool."

"Not a tall guy with blond hair?"

The less tall guy with black hair shook his head. "Is this to do with that rapist who shot two cops and escaped earlier today?" He didn't wait for an answer, just continued, "Cool. Just wait till I tell the guys!"

He scurried off before Ty could ask him anything else. Ty closed the door and shook his head. "Idiot."

"At least he didn't see anybody lurking outside."

I reached for the pizza box. Ty handed it to me. "If somebody's lurking, you don't usually see them. That's the point."

"Details, details." I put the box in the middle of the bed and opened it. "Can we risk a little bit of light, do you think? It's going to be hard to eat without it." Not to mention drink.

He hesitated. "If we sit on the floor."

The hard tile floor.

"Why?"

"Because he'll assume we're sitting on the bed or in the chairs," Ty said. "So he'll aim higher. If we're sitting on the floor, we might be below his target range."

"Or he might shoot us in the head. I feel safer up here." Not to mention that my butt was more comfortable. "I'll do without the light, thank you."

Ty sighed. "I'll turn on the light in the bathroom and crack the door a tiny bit. Just enough so we can see."

"Thank you. Do we have cups?"

"No," Ty said. "We'll have to share the bottle."

Wonderful. And we didn't have plates, so we'd have to eat the pizza straight out of the box. But at least that didn't continually involve putting my lips where Ty's had been, and vice versa.

He turned the bathroom light on and pulled the door shut

until there was a tiny sliver of light coming through the crack, just enough to see what we were doing.

"You know, Cassie," he told me when he came back toward the bed, which was only about three steps away, "we've swapped saliva before."

"And you make it sound so romantic, too." Although I admit my breath caught a little as he climbed onto the bed and headed for me. Before he got there, though, he put his back against the headboard next to me.

He chuckled. "You enjoyed it."

I couldn't very well deny that. He was a very good kisser.

But I didn't want to talk about that. "Why were you asking me about our trip to the hospital?"

"Wanted to hear your impressions," Ty said, grabbing a piece of pizza out of the box and biting into it. He swallowed and added, "You never finished telling me what you thought."

"I think I'd like to kill whoever hurt Juan. And I feel really bad for Martoni." He couldn't be any older than Ty, and now it sounded like his career might be over. He might never be the same. That's a tough thing to happen at our age.

"What about Sullivan?" Ty asked.

"He seems like he'll be all right. I guess getting shot in the leg isn't as big a deal as being shot in the stomach."

"Nowhere near as bad. Unless the bullet nicks an artery. Then you can bleed out just as quickly." He reached for another piece of pizza, having inhaled the first in a couple of bites.

I shot him a sideways glance. "Have you ever...?"

He shook his head. "No, I've managed to avoid that particular experience."

Good.

"So far."

Right. I grimaced.

"Knowing that it might happen is part of the job," Ty said. "But the truth is, it doesn't happen that often. You just hear about it when it does, so it seems like it happens more than it actually does." He shrugged. "Anyway. Sullivan."

"He seemed a little nervous. Like he was afraid Enrique would blame him for what happened. But I thought it was nice of him to ask about Juan."

"Sure," Ty said.

I wrinkled my brows. "What does that mean?"

"What?"

"That 'sure' didn't sound like a sure."

"That's because I'm not sure."

"About what?"

"I think one of them let Stan go," Ty said. "I just don't know which one. And I think that same person may have beat up Juan."

For a second, I didn't know what to say. And I couldn't have said it, even if I knew. Then I found my voice again. "Why? Juan didn't have anything to do with anything."

"No," Ty said, "but if he hadn't been attacked, Enrique and I would have been at the Courthouse today. He would have been riding herd on Sullivan and Martoni."

Yes, but... "You're not really saying that someone hurt Juan just to make sure Ricky—and maybe you—were otherwise occupied when they planned to release Stan, are you?"

He shrugged. "It's possible. I can't imagine any other reason why someone would hurt him."

I could, and told him so. "There are lots of reasons why someone might hurt someone else. It was dark and he was walking alone in a part of town where there aren't as many people as on Duval. Someone might have decided to take his wallet. A random robbery. And when Juan fought back—which I assume he did—things got out of hand. Was his wallet missing?"

Ty nodded. "But that doesn't prove anything. If I wanted to attack someone and make it look like a random robbery, I'd take the wallet, too."

Well, yes. "Someone might have attacked him because he was gay. Gay-bashing happens."

And he had looked especially well-groomed last night.

Besides, when I'd spoken to him, it hadn't sounded like he tried to keep his sexual preferences a secret. A lot of people in Key West probably know.

"No question about it," Ty agreed.

"Or someone might have attacked him because he's Hispanic. Hate-crimes against Hispanics are on the rise."

Ty nodded again. "Or someone could have done it to make sure Enrique had other things on his mind the day they planned to let Stan go."

Yes, but...

I shook my head. I had no idea why I'd rather have Juan hurt because someone wanted him hurt, than because they just wanted a distraction for Enrique. Juan was just as hurt either way, so it wasn't like it mattered. And in a way, being beaten up for being gay, or for being Hispanic, was even worse than being beaten up as a means to keep his brother distracted and away from the Courthouse.

"So you think either Sullivan or Martoni is dirty," I said eventually. And I didn't frame it as a question.

Ty hesitated. "I don't know that I'd go that far. There might be circumstances we don't know about. But I think one of them opened the handcuffs and gave Stan the means to get away. I just don't know which one."

"Are you leaning toward one?"

"No," Ty said. "There's not enough evidence one way or the other. They were both there. Both of them had keys to the handcuffs. Sullivan could have unlocked them when he checked them before putting Stan in the back of the car, and Martoni could have unlocked them when they stopped and he opened the door to the back seat. Sullivan was in the front; he couldn't have seen what Martoni did behind him."

I nodded.

"Carmen mentioned that Sullivan tolerated Stan in school, so their relationship goes back farther, but Stan and Martoni probably worked together long enough to become friends, too."

Probably. "Martoni's injury is a lot worse than Sullivan's. Does that mean it's more likely that Sullivan's guilty, since Stan wouldn't want to hurt his friend?"

"I don't think we can assume that," Ty said. "I doubt Stan has many qualms about hurting people, no matter who they are. And it might have been sheer luck that Sullivan didn't get hurt worse."

True.

"Or, if Martoni helped him, he had incentive to want to silence Martoni, since Martoni might know what his plans are. So in that sense, it's more suspicious that Martoni is the one who almost died."

In the sliver of light from the bathroom, I could see one half of his face quite well. The other half was in shadow.

"You know," I told the part of him I could see, "I wouldn't want to live in your head. It must be a complicated, unpleasant place."

He smiled faintly. "Sorry."

"Don't worry about it. I just find it a little creepy that you can think like that."

He made a sound that was most likely a puff of laughter, but which could have been a snort. "It's—"

"Your job. I know."

I took another slice of pizza from the box and got busy eating.

When the box was empty, Ty moved that and the empty bottle to the floor, and folded the blanket back. In the process, he bumped me off the bed.

"You could just tell me to leave because it's bedtime," I told him.

"I don't want you to leave."

"I'm not sleeping with you!"

"Who said anything about sleeping?" Ty wanted to know. "I'm not leaving you in your room alone all night, Cassie. We're staying together. And it may as well be here." He shrugged.

"Not like we haven't shared a bed before."

No. But that was when we were sleeping together. Now I was looking at a long night of lying next to him but unable to touch.

Not that I imagined he'd mind if I touched. He's a guy. Guys are happy to have sex, even if it's with ex-girlfriends they're just protecting from escaped criminals and don't expect to see again after the weekend is over.

"I love you, Ty," I told him, and realized just a second too late what I was saying, "but you're such a guy."

He grinned. "I think I'll take that as a compliment. You don't mind if I get comfortable, do you?"

He didn't wait for me to answer, just began unbuttoning his shirt. One button at a time, closer and closer to the waistband. I'd seen him naked before, so it wasn't like this was anything new, but there was something about this impromptu striptease that glued my tongue to the roof of my mouth.

I think he must have known it, because he took his time shrugging the shirt off his shoulders and letting it slither to the floor. His hands dropped to the button of the pants. "Now's the time to turn around."

"Not sure I want to turn around," I confessed.

"If you want a good night's sleep tonight, you might want to reconsider."

Sleep's overrated. And with Stan out there, possibly lurking in the hibiscus bushes beyond the pool area, sleep would be hard to come by anyway.

Then again, did I really want to get involved with Ty again?

Sure, I could tell myself it would just be one night. For old times' sake and all that. We were stuck in a motel room together and nature was taking its course.

But I knew the truth. If I slept with him tonight, I wouldn't want to let him go in the morning. I'd get sucked right back into caring for him again.

Hell, I'd never stopped.

He smiled, obviously watching the thoughts chase each

other across my face. "Turn around, Cassie. If we do this again, I want you to be sure. And you're not."

I hesitated, I admit it. Part of me wanted him badly. Part of me wanted to try again, because the last three months without him had been lonely. And it wasn't like I'd stopped worrying about his safety. I'd just worried from farther away and with less information about what he might be doing.

But part of me also knew I wasn't ready. So I got up and turned my back. "I'll have to sleep in my underwear."

"No problem," Ty said from behind my back. I could hear the sound of his zipper going down, a rasp of tiny teeth. "I usually do."

We'd ended up sleeping naked more times than not, actually, but I wasn't about to go there.

So I slipped out of the eyelet dress I had put on this morning—it felt like a year ago—and hung it carefully over the back of the single chair. I'd have to put it on again when I got up tomorrow. Hopefully Ty would let me go to my room then, so I could change into something else.

By the time I turned back to the bed, he had already slipped under the covers. "C'mon," he told me. "I won't bite."

"You told me that last year, too."

"And I didn't. Did I?" He lifted the blanket.

I hesitated for another second, but there was really nothing else I could do. So I crept in next to him and put my head on the pillow.

And there I lay, as stiffly as an effigy on a tombstone, aware of every tiny movement and sound he made. The rustle of the blankets, the slide of the sheets across his skin, the whisper of movement when his hair brushed the pillow. It was a little longer now than the last time I'd seen him, like he hadn't taken the time to have it cut since leaving Chicago.

"Go to sleep, Cassie," he told me. "I can hear the gears moving from over here."

"Your hair's longer."

"So is yours. Go to sleep." He turned over on his stomach.

"I'm a little scared," I told him.

"I won't let anything happen to you." His voice was drowsy. "I promise."

"What if he tries to get in here in the middle of the night?"

There was no need to specify who 'he' was.

"I'll shoot him," Ty murmured.

"The gun's handy?"

"'s under my pillow."

"You're joking."

He sighed. "Go to sleep, Cassie. I've got this."

Fine. I folded my arms over my chest and stared at the ceiling. If I fell asleep, I'd find myself snuggling up to Ty before I knew it, and that was the last thing either of us needed.

CHAPTER
Nine

I woke up snuggled up to Ty, with my nose buried in his throat, my hands against his chest, and my legs tangled with his. I'd woken up that way every morning for six months last year, so I knew what to expect. I knew what the object poking me in the stomach was, too.

"Good morning," Ty said. He sounded wide awake. No surprise there.

"Unh," I answered. My eyelashes felt like they had weights glued to them. It was warm in the bed, while the air conditioning was cold. I was comfortable, and he smelled good. And I had stayed awake long into the night, trying to make it through without letting this happen, but obviously I'd been unsuccessful.

He had an arm around me—not sure whether that had gotten there during sleep, or whether he'd woken up and decided he might as well get in on the action. Either way, his hand was splayed against my lower back, a couple of fingertips actually underneath the elastic on my panties, and now he pressed me a little closer. "I've been here before."

Yes, he had. This was all very familiar.

"I've missed you, Cassie." The words were whispered against my lips.

"I've missed you, too," I admitted, and that's all I had time for before he kissed me.

His lips fitted mine like they belonged there. His tongue swept past my lips, the taste of him achingly familiar. And I was home. Back where I belonged. Nothing else mattered, nothing but his mouth and his hands and his body, the way he touched me and the way he loved me.

My bra was history, and my panties followed a few seconds later. So did his briefs. And we were together again. One.

I felt the tears gather, and tried to blink them back. But he must have tasted them, or just known, because he murmured, "Shhh. It's OK. I'm here."

"That's why I'm crying," I managed.

I could feel his lips curve against my cheek. "I love you, Cassie."

I love you, too.

"I know," I said. He chuckled.

But it had never been about that. I'd never doubted that he loved me. I'd always known I loved him. It was all the rest of it that was the problem. Loving him so much that the thought of anything happening to him filled me with fear. Loving him so much that losing him—voluntarily—after six months seemed easier than losing him after six years, or sixteen, or sixty. When he'd become so much a part of me that I wouldn't know how to go on alone.

I was going to pay for this later. I knew it. But it didn't matter. Not then. All that mattered was Ty. Taking the love he offered and giving my own in return. And I was just about to do that when—

BOOM!

We both jumped. Not easy to do lying down, and especially not easy to do in the middle of what we were doing.

"What the hell—!" Ty said breathlessly.

The sound resolved itself into a barrage of knocking on the door, and then Enrique Fuentes's voice.

"Connor! I know you're in there! Open the damn door!"

Talk about lousy timing.

"Later," Ty told me with a wince, as he removed himself from me and the bed, in that order.

"I'll just go in the bathroom and get dressed," I told him.

He nodded, already in the process of yanking on a pair of jeans. It was my turn to wince as I watched him tuck the evidence of what we'd been doing out of sight behind the zipper. That had to hurt.

"Move," he told me. "He's gonna come through the door as soon as I open it, and you don't want him getting an eyeful of you like that."

No, I didn't. I dug my bra and panties out from the tangle of blankets and sheets, and snagged my dress from the back of the chair. "Stall him long enough that I can get out of sight."

"Not sure he wants to be stalled," Ty said—understandably so, since Enrique was still banging on the door and threatening to shoot the lock off if we, or Ty, didn't respond soon—but he waited until I had ducked into the bathroom and pulled the door mostly shut behind me before he started undoing the locks on the outside door.

I barely had time to step into my panties and pull them up before Enrique burst into the room and let loose with an explosion of Spanish. I know some basic high school Spanish, but I had no hope of following it, and Ty must have found it difficult too, because after a few seconds I heard him say, "Slow down. Slow down! What's going on?"

There was a second's pause, most likely while Enrique switched his brain over from his native Cuban to English. I took the opportunity to slip into my bra and fasten the hooks. Then he was off again.

"He's got her! She's gone!"

"Cassie's right there," Ty said. "In the bathroom."

I opened the door a crack, stuck my hand out, and waved.

Enrique switched to Spanish again, and this time I had no problem following. The comment was blunt, crude, and commented on Ty's lack of morals and intelligence, both.

Then he switched over to English again. "I'm not talking about Cassie."

"Who are you talking about, then?"

"Carmen," Enrique said. "He's taken Carmen."

The next few minutes were a bit of a blur. I dropped the eyelet dress over my head and was still doing up the zipper when I walked out of the bathroom. "What do you mean, he's taken Carmen? Stan's taken Carmen?"

"Who else?" Enrique snarled.

Ty looked confused. "Why would he want Carmen?"

"No idea," Enrique said, halfway between sarcastic and furious. "You obviously don't." He shot me a look that could have peeled the paint off the wall behind me.

Uh-oh.

"Leave Cassie out of it," Ty ordered. And added, more reasonably, "You know we lived together for six months in Chicago."

"So this is just picking up where you left off?"

Enrique shook his head and pinched the bridge of his nose with two fingers. "You know what? I don't give a shit what you do on your own time. If you make a habit of sleeping with witnesses you're protecting, that's your business. Carmen's mine. And she's gone."

"How?" Ty wanted to know.

"How the fuck do I know? I wasn't there!"

"So how do you know Stan took her?" I asked, trying to be the voice of reason. "Maybe she went for a run, or something."

The both looked at me like they suspected I'd lost my mind. I guess Carmen didn't run.

"Maybe she went to the hospital to see Juan," I said. "Maybe she spent the night with a friend because she didn't want to be alone."

There was a beat of silence. Then—

"Do me a favor, Cassie," Enrique said.

"Sure."

"Don't try to help."

Ouch. I sniffed. "Tell you what. I'll go to my own room, so I can change out of this dress and this underwear, since I wore it all day yesterday. I'd like to brush my teeth, too. And I'm sure Ty would like a couple minutes alone in the bathroom. And you could use some time to calm down so you don't bite people's heads off for trying to help. Then we'll figure out what happened and where she is, and go find her."

I didn't wait for either of them to agree or disagree, just grabbed my purse from the floor beside the door and headed out. If Stan had Carmen, then he was busy with her, and I wasn't in any danger.

Except Ty must not agree, because there was a minor explosion behind me. "Go after her, dammit!"

"If he's got Carmen, he's not going to bother with Cassie," Enrique said—not the most flattering sentiment, really, even if I'd just thought the exact same thing myself—but he must have changed his mind, because a few seconds later I heard his footsteps behind me. "Cassie! Wait!"

I didn't. But I did slow down a little so he could catch up. And by the time I'd dug my key out of my purse and inserted it in the lock of the door, it was Enrique who went through first, gun drawn.

The room was empty, of course. I hadn't expected anything else. Unflattering it may be, but Enrique was right: if Stan had grabbed Carmen, why would he bother with me?

It took me a minute to change into clean underwear, a pair of jeans, and a T-shirt. It took another thirty seconds to brush my teeth. Usually I do the recommended ninety, but Enrique was standing outside the door tapping his foot, so I had incentive to hurry. I bundled my hair into a messy ponytail—unintentionally messy, since I didn't take time to comb first, but nobody had to know that. And then I stuffed my feet into a pair of sneakers—just in case I had to run away from someone, or toward them—and headed back out. "I'm ready."

"Let's go." Ty was already there. I wondered whether he'd taken the time to put on a pair of briefs, or whether he was still commando under the jeans.

And then I told myself to stop thinking about it, since it was distracting, and the last thing any of us needed right now was a distraction.

Enrique had brought the car, of course, and I crawled into the back seat again while he and Ty took the front. They were both armed today. Enrique always was—the gun was part of his uniform of tailored suit and tie—and I saw the handle peek out from Ty's waistband when he got into the car. I hoped he was right about Glocks taking effort to fire, because I'd hate for him to shoot himself in the butt.

"Can you tell us what happened?" he asked when we were inside the car with the doors locked and the air conditioning going. "You dropped Carmen off at your parents' house last night for dinner, and then you took Cassie and me here."

Enrique nodded. "And then I went back to work. The tip line kept getting calls, and people kept saying they'd seen Stan. The darker it got, the more likely it was that he was actually out there somewhere, so I spent most of the night driving around, checking out tips."

"Did you get any sleep?" I asked, worried. He was driving me and Ty around; if he hadn't slept at all, what were the chances that we'd get through the day without crashing the car?

"Couple hours. More than I get sometimes." He went back to the events of last night, or this morning. "I never saw him. Whether he'd been there at all, or whether the people who thought they saw him were wrong, I'm not sure."

"What were some of the sightings?" Ty asked.

Enrique sighed. "The cemetery again. Walking down Duval talking to himself. Sitting at a corner table in Sloppy

Joe's Bar."

"That last one was probably the liquor talking," Ty said. "Either that, or someone thought it would be funny to watch a SWAT team in full riot gear come into Sloppy Joe's."

Enrique nodded. "I didn't respond to that one. They know Stan at Sloppy Joe's. If he was there, someone would have called me."

"So about Carmen..."

Enrique closed his eyes for a moment. I was about to tell him to open them again when he did. "I caught a couple hours sleep and a shower between two and five, basically. And then I stopped by my mom's house for breakfast. My dad goes to work early, so I knew they'd be up. I wanted to know when they were planning to go to the hospital."

Ty and I both nodded.

"There were *tostadas* and *café con leche*, so I took a couple minutes to sit and eat. And then I asked why Carmen wasn't up, when all the rest of us were."

"Does she live with your parents?" I asked.

Enrique shook his head. "She has her own place. But I thought she'd stay the night. It was late when we got there, and she knew Stan was out there somewhere..."

"But she left?" Ty said.

"*Mamá* said she got a text message. I thought maybe—" He glanced at Ty, who shook his head. "I checked her apartment. It was empty. And I knocked on Cassie's door. When she didn't answer, I figured she was with you. And if you were with Cassie..."

He didn't finish the sentence. He didn't have to. If Ty had been with me, he hadn't been with Carmen.

"So where is she?" I asked. "I mean, just because she isn't at home, or at your parents' house," or with Ty, "doesn't mean Stan has her. Maybe she couldn't sleep and went to the hospital early. Maybe she spent the night with a friend. Maybe a guy she knew made a booty call, and since Ty turned her down, she wanted someone to want her, so she went to meet him."

There was a moment of silence. Enrique didn't say anything. Ty grimaced.

"I found this," Enrique said. "Stuck between the door and the jamb at her place. Like a fucking calling card."

He pulled something out of his pocket. A small, white rectangle inside a clear plastic envelope.

It really was a calling card. Or a business card, rather. Just like the one had been leaning up against the vase of flowers in my room three days ago. It had the logo of the Key West Police on the front, with its bright yellow sun, and the slogan Protecting & Serving Paradise in cursive along the bottom. Just above was an officer's name and contact information.

Or an ex-officer. Stanley Laszlo.

"He left this on her door?" Ty asked, turning it over in his hands. I didn't want to touch it, even through the plastic. I had a feeling it would make me feel contaminated.

Enrique nodded.

"Could mean one of two things. He grabbed her, and wants us to know it. Or he was there and didn't find her, but he wants her to know he can come back anytime he wants."

"Stalker," Enrique muttered.

"We already knew he'd been obsessed with her for years." Ty's voice was calm. He put the business card down in the console between the seats. "This just proves he still is."

Enrique's hands tightened on the wheel. "So what do we do now?"

"First we figure out where she is. Then we deal with what needs dealing with. I assume you've tried to call her?"

"All morning," Enrique said. "Her phone's off." He added, before Ty or I could, "Doesn't mean anything either way. She could have run out of juice and forgotten to charge it. Or he could have turned it off."

"So she's not at home," I said. "She's not at your parents' house. I assume you've talked to your other siblings. Have you checked with the hospital?"

Enrique nodded. "She hasn't been there this morning."

"Does she have a job?"

"She's a waitress," Enrique said. "She has the week off for the trial."

"So she probably wouldn't be at work. Have you checked anyway?"

"It's a bar. They won't be open until ten."

Because the bars opened at the crack of dawn in Party Central.

"Friends?" I said, a bit desperately. "Does she have any?"

"She grew up here. Of course she does."

"Have you checked with them?" Ty asked, hearing—or sensing—my frustration. He glanced at me over the back of the seat and winked.

I smiled back, and then I felt a little guilty. Here I was, googly-eyed (again) over this guy I liked, while Carmen could be tied to a bed in Stan's personal dungeon. Or locked in a mausoleum at the Key West Cemetery. Or dead.

"Have you checked the cemetery?" I asked.

"The cemetery?"

"He seemed to like it there. It's where he took me. And Jeanine, one of the other girls. And it's where Juan was found."

"That was a coincidence," Enrique said.

"Maybe not."

He looked at me in the rearview mirror. "What do you mean?"

I sat back against the seat. "I think I'll let Ty explain this one."

"Thanks a lot," Ty said, and turned to Enrique.

CHAPTER
Ten

"That's crazy," Enrique said after Ty had gone over his reasoning for why Juan had been attacked. "Nobody would do something like that."

"Stan would. Juan's your brother. He'd see it as getting back at you for arresting him."

"That's crazy," Enrique said again, but with a bit less conviction. "And anyway, Stan was still locked up the night Juan..."

"That's the whole point," Ty said. "He needed you and me out of the way so he could escape."

"But that's crazy."

"Maybe," Ty said. "But it's logical. And too much of a coincidence otherwise."

Enrique thought for a moment. "He could have heard about it and decided to take advantage of you and me being gone. Sullivan or Martoni could have been talking about what happened when they picked him up that morning. And by the afternoon he had decided to make his move."

"Sure. It just seems it would take a little more planning than that. And some help."

Enrique was quiet.

"So which of your officers do you think opened the handcuffs?"

"Neither of them," Enrique said.

"Someone did. Unless whoever put them on in the first place didn't do a good job. But Sullivan said he checked them when they picked Stan up. So if whoever put the cuffs on left them open, he's either a liar or incompetent."

"He's not incompetent," Enrique said.

Ty and I both waited, but he didn't continue.

"Martoni?" Ty said.

"Not incompetent, either."

"Is either of them a liar?"

Enrique scowled out the windshield at the traffic. "If what you're saying is true, one of them must be."

"Is either of them gay?" I asked.

Enrique looked shocked. "If he is, he hasn't told me. We don't talk about that."

"Don't ask, don't tell? I thought they did away with that." I glanced at Ty for confirmation. He shrugged.

"Someone's sexual orientation is nobody's business but his own," Enrique said primly. And added, "Unless he likes kids. Then he's my business."

Of course. "Juan was meeting someone the night he was attacked. He said it wasn't a date, but he dressed up for it."

Enrique looked sick. "You're saying one of my cops pretended to be gay and asked my brother on a date so he could beat him up?"

"He may not have been pretending. He may just be so deep in the closet you don't know about it. But yes, that's what I'm saying."

"I'm gonna kill the bastard," Enrique said. His hands tightened around the steering wheel until his knuckles stood out against the golden skin.

"How about we just arrest him?" Ty suggested, as the same time as I said, "We have to figure out who he is first."

"And find Carmen," Ty added.

"Right." Enrique straightened his shoulders, with a sort of mental 'first things first' adjustment of attitude. "Stan's folks lived down here on the right."

He pointed. We were on our way down an overgrown street on the north side of the island, filled with small, low-slung, cinderblock homes, close together. They had front yards not much bigger than one of my textbooks, filled with sand and patches of grass, and there was a palm tree or two in front of practically every house. Some of the houses were painted in happy, tropical colors, like turquoise and yellow and peach, but a lot were just plain white. Some were peeling and looked like they had leprosy.

"They left town a couple years ago," Enrique added, "and since then, Stan's been living here alone. Nobody thought he'd come here yesterday—"

"It's the obvious place."

He nodded. "So we didn't bother to post a guard, since we needed all the manpower we could get for other things. Although of course we checked. He wasn't here. But it won't hurt to check again."

No, it wouldn't. When he pulled the car up to the curb and stopped, I reached for my door handle. Only to have Ty turn in his seat. "Stay."

I subsided, but not without a scowl. "What am I, a dog?"

"I'm not risking you out there. Stay in the car with the doors locked and the windows up. We get paid to take down dangerous criminals. You don't."

At the moment, it was almost impossible to imagine such a thing as a dangerous criminal. The sky was a brilliant blue, the sun was beaming down, the green palm fronds were rustling in the breeze, and everything looked idyllic. The idea of a gunfight in the middle of all this was ludicrous.

"OK," I said, mostly because I figured they wouldn't find

him here anyway. He really would have to be stupid to come here, and I didn't think he was. "I'll wait."

"Don't leave the car." Ty opened his door.

"She can't," Enrique told him. "Police car, remember? The child locks are engaged."

Child locks. Great.

He was right, though. My door was locked, and stayed locked, no matter how hard I yanked on the handle. Now that was just insulting.

"Flak vests are in the trunk," Enrique added.

I watched as they both went around to the back of the car. Then the trunk popped and I couldn't see anything but burgundy metal for a minute before one of them slammed it shut again. By then, they had both put on black vests with the word POLICE across the back, and lots of Velcro straps. Ty had his gun in his hand, and as I watched, Enrique pulled his from the holster under his arm. He'd stripped out of his suit jacket and down to his shirt, and looked a bit ridiculous with the bulky black vest on top of the dressy pants and crisp shirt. There was nothing ridiculous about the gun, though, or about the way they approached the house through the gate in the small wall surrounding it, before splitting off to the left and right and slithering along with their back against the walls. Every time one of them had to pass a window, he pulled the gun up and aimed it at the window before darting past. And then it was back to the wall and sideways movement like a crab again.

It was a little like watching a cop show on TV—*Hawaii 5-0*, with all the palm trees—but a lot more personal, and nerve-wracking.

Ty went around the corner on the right first. A few seconds later, Enrique disappeared around the corner on the left and into the shadowy carport. I strained my ears, wondering whether I could risk opening the window just an inch to see what I could hear. But Ty had told me to keep the windows up, and I didn't want him mad at me. And anyway, if the child locks had been engaged, the window locks probably had, too.

I checked, just in case. Yep.

Nothing happened, though. No shots were fired. It seemed like an eternity passed, but by the clock it was only about four minutes before they both came around the corner again, together this time, walking normally with guns lowered. Obviously Stan hadn't been there.

"Nothing?" I asked when they were back inside the car. They hadn't bothered to take the bulletproof vests off, so I guess they figured they might need them again.

Ty shook his head. "No sign he's been, either."

I glanced at the house. The roof was practically flat, the pitch no more than two feet from the peak to the gutter, so obviously there was no attic. "I don't suppose there's a basement?"

"No basement," Enrique said. "These little houses are sitting on concrete slabs."

So that was that, then. Stan wasn't here. "I assume someone has spoken to the neighbors."

"You assume correctly," Enrique said. "Someone went up and down this whole street yesterday. Nobody had seen Stan. Several people said they'd call us if they did."

"And you trust them?"

"No reason not to," Enrique said.

Right. They probably didn't want Stan on the loose any more than we did. "Where to next?"

"He never had many friends to begin with," Enrique said, starting the car, "and after what he did, he has less. Carmen gave me a list of people she thought he might turn to. We checked with all of them yesterday and didn't get the impression anyone would help him should he show up. Especially with an unconscious woman over his shoulder."

"Sullivan and Martoni are both still in the hospital. Could he be using one of their places?"

"It's worth checking," Enrique said and pulled away from the curb.

Key West is a small place, and it was only a few minutes— no more than a couple of blocks—before we drove into an apartment complex in the same neighborhood as Stan's parents' house. It consisted of a half dozen buildings which had seen better days: a little tired-looking, with the bright tropical paint faded.

"Who lives here?" Ty wanted to know.

"Dave Sullivan. You see D-building?"

D-building was, not surprisingly, between C and E. We pulled up in front of D-11, where the parking spot was empty. "I don't think he'd risk taking her to a place where there are neighbors on both sides," Ty said, looking around.

Enrique shook his head. "Probably not. But we'll check anyway." He opened his door. "If nothing else, maybe we'll figure out which one of them opened those handcuffs yesterday."

Ty nodded and reached for his own door handle.

"Let me guess," I said. "Stay."

"Please." Ty pushed the door open. "It's for your own protection."

"You said yourself he isn't likely to be here."

"That doesn't mean I'm willing to take chances." He checked his gun before swinging his legs out of the car. "I just don't want anything to happen to you, Cassie."

He didn't wait for me to answer, just slammed the door behind him. Enrique locked it with the remote, and they walked off.

This time there was no sneaking around corners. They just walked up to the front of the townhouse and into the little screened porch that protected the front door. Enrique got down on one knee in front of the lock while Ty kept an eye out for any activity.

It took Enrique less than thirty seconds to open the lock. I have no idea whether he had a universal master or whether he was just that good with a lock pick, but they disappeared inside.

It wasn't a very big place, so it was only a few minutes before they came out again. A couple of people came and went in that time, but no one I recognized, and no one who even noticed me sitting there.

"Nothing?" I asked when they were back in the car.

Ty shook his head. "No Carmen. And no sign anyone's been here."

"Did you look around?"

"Can't," Enrique said, holstering his pistol before starting the car. "Not without a warrant."

"You went inside without a warrant."

"We thought we might have cause. Carmen might have been inside, unable to scream. But I can't go through Sully's stuff without a warrant."

He sounded frustrated.

"So no idea whether he was Stan's helper?"

He shook his head. "The calendar didn't have 'Help Stan escape' written on yesterday's date. And I didn't see anything else in plain view that would give me reason to suspect he was."

"So where do we go now? Martoni's place?"

Ty nodded. "May as well. If it wasn't Sullivan who helped him, it had to be Martoni."

Enrique muttered something. I thought it might have been "I hope not," but it was impossible to know for sure, and I wasn't going to ask him to repeat it. If he'd wanted me to hear, he would have said it out loud to begin with. Still, I got the impression that maybe he liked Martoni a little better than he liked Sullivan. Or that he would be a little more upset if Stan's helper turned out to be Martoni.

"We can't assume that the place he's chosen to go to ground in has anything to do with who helped him escape," Ty said. "This—" he gestured out the window, at the rows of townhouses and cars, "isn't a good place to keep a hostage. There are too many people, and the walls are too thin. A single family house would be better. A large property would be even better."

"Not a lot of those around here," Enrique said.

I said it again, since nobody had really listened the first time. "What about the islands? There are private islands around here, right? Some of them have structures on them. Could he be in one of those?"

"That would mean he'd have to either drag Carmen, kicking and screaming, through Key West to where he had a boat. Or, if she was unconscious, he'd have to carry her. She isn't a small woman, and he isn't a particularly big guy. Tall, but not heavily built. He'd find it heavy going after a couple of blocks."

An incongruous mental picture of Stan pushing a wheelbarrow with Carmen's unconscious body down Duval popped into my brain, and I shook my head. "If he could get her out there, nobody would—" I bit back the words 'hear her scream' before they tumbled out of my mouth, "—know where they were," I substituted lamely.

Enrique shot me a look in the rearview mirror, and Ty rolled his eyes.

I blushed. "Sorry."

Enrique shook his head. "Don't be. You're right. If he could get her to one of the islands, he could do anything he wanted to her, and we'd never find them. I'll tell the Coast Guard to pay special attention to islands with structures."

"But it's more likely they're somewhere around here," Ty said. "He's not going to want to risk being caught again, and the more he has to walk around in public, the more likely it is someone will see him. He'd have wanted to get under cover as quickly as possible last night. It was late, but there were still people out."

Yes, indeed. Key West is the other city that never sleeps, especially around Spring Break.

On the face of it, Martoni's house had more potential. It sat closer to the south end of the island, and backed up to some sort of nature preserve. The houses were a bit bigger in this part of town, and sat a little farther apart. Many of them had fences surrounding the properties. The cars were fancier and newer, and the grass was a little greener. I guess maybe the folks on the north side had better things to do than water their lawns. Either that, or they didn't want to increase their water bills.

Ty whistled. "Nice."

"Martoni comes from money," Enrique said, stopping the car outside a two story house behind a fence. "He went to college and got a degree before he joined the PD. Stan joined straight out of high school, and Sully spent a couple years in the army first."

"He doesn't live here alone, does he?" The house was rather big for one person.

"It's his family's vacation place," Enrique said. "He isn't local. He used to come here with his family for vacations and decided he'd like to live here. And the house was just sitting empty, so he moved in. His folks don't mind. There's plenty of room for them when they want to come for a visit."

Plenty of room for Stan and Carmen, too.

"Are his folks here now?"

Enrique shook his head. "They live up north somewhere, Massachusetts or Maine, and they're still working. They usually come down for the summers. Sometimes for Christmas, too, if Cody's scheduled to work, but if he's off, he flies up there. Says he likes to see snow for Christmas."

The Martoni family sounded nice. And the house was certainly lovely.

"You've told them what happened, right?"

"Of course," Enrique said. "They're flying down today. Should be in around one, although I guess they'll be going straight to the hospital."

I would imagine.

"So if Stan's using this place, he'll have to get out this morning. Surely he must realize that as badly hurt as Martoni is, his parents would want to come see him."

"You'd think," Enrique said and opened his door. "Ready?" That last one wasn't directed at me. Ty nodded and turned. "I know," I said, before he could say it. "Stay in the car."

He nodded.

Here we go again.

I watched them pass through the gate and then split up, one to the left and one to the right. Both had their guns out and ready, and both were slithering through the underbrush like Natty Bumppo.

I watched until they were gone, and then I leaned back against the seat. It would be a longer wait this time. It was a pretty big house, more than twice the size of the Laszlo family's home, and they'd have to go through the place from top to bottom. Here, there might be a basement, and there might also be an attic. There was certainly a second floor, and enough pitch to the roof for a third.

I might have been sitting there for two minutes, maybe, when there was a loud popping sound. I jerked upright, and leaned toward the window.

Gunshot?

Please don't let it be a gunshot!

A few seconds later, a figure came flying through the yard. At first I thought it was Enrique, because of the flashes of a white shirt I could see between the bushes and trees.

But then he came bounding over the low wall separating the yard from the street, and skidded to a stop for a second, and I saw it wasn't Enrique at all. He was tall and gangly, with a little head on top of a long neck, and a beaky nose that made him look like a stork.

Stan!

I sank down in the seat as far as I could go, and hoped he wouldn't see me.

It was idiotic, of course. This was the only car parked at the curb on the whole block, and it was just a few yards away from him. Everyone else had parked in their driveways, or underneath their carports, behind their fences and walls.

While Enrique's unmarked police car was just sitting here, like a giant beacon. *Pick me! Pick me!*

Stan was on it like white on rice. I braced myself to have him yank on the door handle, and maybe try to break the window. What I didn't expect, was for the door to open and for him to slide behind the wheel.

He had a key.

How did he get a key? Enrique had the key. What had he done to Enrique?

I stuffed my knuckles in my mouth and bit down on them so I wouldn't make a sound, still trying to make myself as small as possible so he wouldn't see me curled up in a ball behind his seat.

It wasn't that I wanted to get kidnapped, really, but I couldn't get out. If I could be small and quiet enough back here, maybe he wouldn't notice me. Maybe he'd just drive somewhere and abandon the car, and wouldn't ever realize I'd been here.

The engine roared to life. Stan yanked the gear shift down and we leaped away from the curb and took off down the street with a squeal of tires. I did my best to brace myself so I wouldn't rattle around and give away the fact that I was here. But I risked a glance out the window, and saw a figure come tearing out of the yard and stop in the middle of the street, feet apart and braced, gun raised.

But instead of firing at the car, he just stood there. And I knew why. Ty knew I was in here, and rather than risking my life by shooting at the car, he was letting Stan get away.

The only problem was, he had me with him. And Ty had no way of following.

He must be kicking himself for insisting that I had to stay in the car.

We squealed around a corner, and Stan reached up to adjust the rearview mirror.

"Hello, Cassie," he told me. "Long time, no see."

CHAPTER
Eleven

"You won't get away with this," I told him. I don't know why, since it made me sound like the stupid heroine in a stupid movie.

"I've gotten away with it so far," Stan informed me, which was certainly true. However—

"So far is less than twenty-four hours. And you've lost Carmen."

"I didn't want Carmen," Stan said, as he maneuvered the car around a corner at warp speed. I don't know why. It wasn't like Ty or Enrique had any way of following. Enrique may not even be alive anymore.

"What did you do to Detective Fuentes?" I asked.

"Hit him over the head and took his car keys," Stan answered.

"Is he still alive?"

Stan shrugged. "One less raft monkey won't matter."

It would matter to me. And to Ty. And it would obviously matter to the rest of the Fuenteses. And Enrique might have a girlfriend somewhere, to whom it would matter. The Key West PD might not be too happy, either. Nor the state of Florida, come to that.

It would do no good to tell Stan any of that, though.

"Why didn't you want Carmen?" I asked instead. "You took the trouble to grab her. You must have wanted her last night."

"That was when I thought I could get both Fuentes and Agent Connor by grabbing her," Stan said, taking another corner on two wheels. At this rate, we'd be pulled over by a traffic cop long before anyone actually came in pursuit of us. "The way Connor was all over her at the trial, I figured he'd care what happened to her."

"Of course he cares what happened to her. He was back there. Didn't you see him?"

"He spent the night with you," Stan said.

Well, yes. But— "How do you know that?"

"She told me," Stan said.

"Did you hurt her?"

I didn't really think about the words before I asked them. Once they were out of my mouth I kind of wished I hadn't. I wasn't sure I wanted to know the answer. For all I knew right now, Carmen was alive and well and really grateful for being rescued, not lying lifeless in a pool of her own blood in the Martonis' basement.

"Just a little," Stan said, which didn't sound all that good.

I looked out the window. Houses and palm trees were flashing by, between occasional glimpses of azure sea. "Where are we going?"

"If I told you that, I'd have to kill you," Stan said, and chuckled merrily at his own wit.

"Aren't I going to find out where we're going when we get there?"

It seemed like maybe he hadn't thought of that. "Can't you just tell me now?" I added, crossing my fingers. If he did, maybe I'd be able to get my phone out of my pocket without him realizing it, and I could send a message to Ty.

"Somewhere private," Stan said, which didn't sound so good, either.

"Ty will find you, you know. Even if it means knocking on every door on the island."

"By then it'll be too late," Stan said, which sounded worst of all. "Now shut up and let me drive."

Fine. I sat back and let the landscape flash by while I thought about my options.

I didn't have many. He had the gun and at least forty or fifty pounds on me. He also had control of the car and a plan. I had nothing. Not even the ability to open my door or my window to save myself if he drove us into the water.

I had my phone, but I was sitting on it, and if I started twisting around in the backseat, Stan would surely notice and wonder what was up. And then he'd take the phone away, and with it, my only link to the rest of the world.

And speaking of twisting around in the backseat... "Congratulations on getting away yesterday. It's a pity you had to shoot your accomplice to do it."

Stan scowled at me in the rearview mirror. "How d'you know that?"

"It was obvious," I said. "You couldn't have opened the handcuffs on your own. Someone had to open them for you. The only question was who."

"Fucking faggot," Stan growled. "Rolled right over on me, didn't he?"

Actually, he hadn't. Whichever of them he was, Sullivan or Martoni. Neither of them had confessed. And neither had struck me as particularly gay, for that matter, but then I hadn't pegged Juan either, until he told me.

But would I be better off letting Stan think that his accomplice—the one he'd shot—had confessed all, or that he was still keeping mum about his role in the escape?

And did it matter either way?

I was still trying to figure it out—quickly, and without

letting on that I was trying to figure it out—when my back pocket vibrated. A second later it rang.

Stan's eyes whipped to me in the rearview mirror.

"My phone's ringing," I told him as I dug for it.

"Don't answer it!"

What was he going to do, shoot me?

I looked at the readout. "It's Ty." No way was I not answering that. I'd risk getting shot. At least I'd hear Ty's voice again.

Yeah, stupid sentiment. But still, I punched the button and put the phone to my ear. "Hello?"

"Let me talk to him," Ty said, his voice set to grim. He didn't even bother to ask me how I was. I guess he assumed, since I was still able to answer my phone, that I was all right. And of course he knew that I'd been in the back of the car, and Stan had gotten into the front, and he may just surmise that Stan hadn't bothered to stop the car to deal with me yet. It felt like an eternity, but per the dashboard clock, we'd only been driving for four minutes or so.

"I'm going to put you on speaker," I told him, since I didn't want to give up the phone, and since Stan was driving the car with one hand and keeping a tight grip on the gun with the other.

If I gave him the phone, he might put the gun down. But I wouldn't have any opportunity to get at it, and I would have given up my phone. I'd rather keep hold of the phone, in case it turned out to be useful. Part of me—the sentimental part—was loath to give up my lifeline.

"You goddamn effing son of a bitch," Ty began, and then went on to tell Stan, in excruciating detail, exactly what he would do to him if he—Stan—harmed a hair on my head.

It was a bit surprising, to be honest. Ty doesn't usually lose his temper, and I'd never heard him lose it this way. The FBI expects its agents to behave professionally, with a certain sense of decorum, and there was nothing professional about this.

At first Stan seemed to find it humorous, but as the threats and curses went on, becoming more and more inventive, the grin slipped off his face to be replaced by a surly and then sulky look.

"Turn it off!" he ordered after a minute or so.

I pulled the phone back into the backseat and turned off the speaker. "Ty? He doesn't want to listen to you anymore."

Ty took a breath. Meanwhile, Stan growled, "I said, turn it off!"

"I did turn it off," I told him. "You can't hear him anymore, can you?"

"You OK?" Ty asked, as Stan got even more angry.

"I meant, turn it all the way off!"

"So far," I told Ty. "We've been driving this whole time." To Stan I said, "In a minute."

"Now!" He turned around in his seat and pointed the gun at me.

"We'll crash," I told him. "There's a car up ahead."

He turned back around without shooting me. *Good.*

"Where are you?" Ty wanted to know.

I glanced out the window. "No idea. I've never been here before." Somewhere on the north side, judging from the turns we'd made. "Near water. A marina. Boats."

"Shut the fucking phone off!" Stan bellowed.

"In a minute. Keep your shirt on."

"He's undressing?" Ty asked tightly.

"No, he's not undressing." *Sheesh.* "He's driving the car. And yelling at me to turn the phone off."

"Don't," Ty said. "Keep talking to me as long as you can without forcing him to hurt you."

No problem. "How's Enrique? And Carmen?"

"Fine," Ty said. "And a little less fine. The ambulance is on the way for Enrique. Stan knocked him unconscious. He'll have a hell of headache when he comes to, and I think he probably has a concussion. But his skull is intact."

Good to know. "And Carmen?"

"Awake and aware. She was tied to the bed in the master bedroom. And this time he didn't bother drugging her."

FINDING *You*

I pressed my lips together. "Is she all right?"

"As all right as can be expected," Ty said. "She's waiting to go in the ambulance with her brother. I'm waiting for someone to bring me a vehicle. Where are you now?"

I glanced out the window again, while in the front seat, Stan was muttering dire threats about what he'd do if I didn't get off the phone immediately. "Same thing. Water on the right, parking lot on the left. Cars and boats."

"Islands?"

I couldn't see any and told him so. Meanwhile, Stan was coming close to losing it. "If you don't turn off the fucking phone right fucking now, I'm gonna fucking shoot you!"

"I better go," I told Ty. "He looks like he means it."

"Don't push him so far that he hurts you."

I doubted that was an option anymore, but I didn't say so. "I love..."

That was all I got out before Stan swung around in the seat and popped off a round. The sound of the shot in the interior of the car was excruciatingly loud, and I think I screamed in sheer surprise. It wasn't so much in terror, because the bullet didn't come close to hitting me.

Or perhaps I shouldn't say that. When it comes to bullets, a hundred yards is a little too close, while this certainly came a lot closer than that. But it buried itself harmlessly in the leather and stuffing of the seat with a small puff of dust, half a foot from my elbow.

We screeched to a stop, and I got thrown forward against the front seat, and then back again against my own. Stan's mouth moved, but I couldn't hear his voice. I could read his lips, though. "Gimme the phone."

The hand he held out got the point across, too. I put the phone into it and watched him lift it to his mouth. I couldn't hear the words this time either, and I saw him only in profile, but I'm pretty sure he said, "That'll be your girlfriend if you call back."

And then he turned the phone off, got out of the car, and

tossed it in the water.

So much for my lifeline to Ty.

I thought about slithering over the seat and making a break for it, but before I could, Stan came stalking back and pulled open the back door. He reached in. I scrabbled over into the far corner and kicked at him, and he grabbed my foot and yanked me out. Then he grabbed me by the arm and yanked me upright.

"I still have a couple bullets left," he told me through the ringing in my ears, as he dug the muzzle of the gun into my side, "so don't do anything stupid."

No, sir. I tried very hard not to do anything at all as we made our way through the parking lot toward the water. But then curiosity got the better of me. "What are we doing here?"

"We're going on a boat," Stan said.

My heart sank. Just like I'd tried to convince Ty and Enrique, the safest way to stay hidden was to go to one of the small islands to the north of us, in the Gulf of Mexico, between the Keys and the mainland. There were dozens of them, from Key West all the way to Marathon, and although the Coast Guard was out in force, they couldn't possibly check them all. He could take me there, do whatever he wanted to me, and then take his time burying the leftovers somewhere isolated, where nobody would find me. My parents would never know what happened to me.

I tried to yank free, but his fingers dug into my arm, and the point of the gun dug into my ribs. I blinked at the tears in my eyes, but they wouldn't go away.

There was a movement to my right, where an older man got out of a car. He went around to the trunk and pulled out a bucket; probably something slimy, like bait.

"Keep walking," Stan said, his voice tight. "One wrong move and I'll shoot you, and then I'll shoot him."

He sounded like he might mean it. I kept walking, even as I shot longing glances at the old guy. He looked up from fiddling with his bucket and watched us move past. I gave him a strained smile, but didn't dare to do anything more.

The pavement gave way to a metal sort of ramp heading down, and then a floating pier. It was made of concrete, but it undulated gently up and down as we walked. All along it, boats bobbed on the water. Sleek, white sailboats with tall masts, powerful speedboats, humble fishing boats, and fancy cabin cruisers with foreign flags on the stern. Several flew the blue Conch Republic flag: a conch shell on top of a sun bracketed by stars, and the words *Conch Republic* above and *We Seceded Where Others Failed* below.

Here and there, people were out on decks doing things. Checking out the weather, enjoying breakfast in the sun, or getting ready to go somewhere. Some of them watched us pass, but nobody said anything. I didn't either. The barrel of the gun digging into my ribs was a powerful deterrent.

Eventually there was nowhere else to go, just the turquoise water of the Gulf of Mexico stretched out in front of us, and I started worrying that Stan was going to toss me in. Surely he wasn't so far gone that he'd shoot me in front of all these witnesses. Was he?

"This way." He yanked on my arm. And that's when I saw the last boat in the marina. It was sitting at the end of the row, bobbing gently up and down.

It looked different from the others. It was white and mint green, and sort of square. More like a raft with a hut on it, surrounded by a railing.

"A houseboat?" I couldn't quite keep the amazement out of my voice. It even had flower pots on the window sill.

Stan didn't answer, just kept me moving. I stumbled along, wondering what would happen if I tried to yank free and throw myself sideways off the pier and into open water.

Stan might shoot at my head when I came back up.

He might hit me.

Or I might drown. I'm from Ohio. Other than Lake Erie to the north, hours from Braxton, Ohio doesn't have that many large, open areas of water. I can swim, but not terribly well. I've spent the past couple of years in Chicago, which might as well be on the beach—the lake looks like an ocean—but it's only warm in Chicago during the summer, and in the winter it's so cold you can ice skate on the lake. I hadn't had much occasion to become a champion swimmer.

Then again, if it was a choice between getting raped and drowning, I'd take my chances in the water.

"Don't even think about it," Stan growled. He took a firmer grip on my arm, the tips of his fingers digging into my skin. I'd have bruises tomorrow.

If I survived until tomorrow.

And if I did, bruises were the least of the injuries I would have to worry about.

"C'mon." He pushed me from the pier on to the moving deck of the boat, and then through the door to the cabin. "In."

I went in.

CHAPTER
Twelve

The interior was dim. There were shades on the big, square windows in the front, and the small windows along each side were no bigger than portholes. The ceiling was low—

"Down," Stan said, giving me a shove toward a staircase. It was only six steps deep—somewhere between three and four feet, maybe—but the ceiling opened up a little once we got down there.

I looked around

Other than the tiny bridge upstairs, a couple of feet of standing space with a wheel, the entire interior of the boat seemed to consist of this one room with a tiny bathroom tacked on at the back. I could see the outline of the toilet bowl through a half-open door. Other than that, this single room served as bedroom, living room, dining room, and kitchen, and it was no bigger than eight by twelve.

A tiny kitchen was tucked in next to the stairs, with a table and two chairs making up the dining area. Against the wall opposite stood the sofa with a small coffee table. And in the opposite corner from that, a queen-sized bed with a tiny nightstand. A chest of drawers served as both wardrobe for the bedroom and TV-stand for the living room, with a couple of feet separating it from either.

The nightstand had a picture on it. Since Stan had released his death grip on my arm and was just guarding the staircase to make sure I didn't make a break for the upstairs and freedom, I walked over to look at it. And found myself staring at the Fuentes family. All of them dark and good-looking and smiling at the camera.

And now Juan was in the hospital and Enrique was on his way there, and God only knew what Stan had done to Carmen, but from what Ty had managed to get out, it sounded like she was due for a trip to the doctor, too. I put the picture back down, shuddering at the thought of the rape kit and the questions she'd have to answer. She'd had no memory of the last time Stan raped her. This time she'd remember every detail for the rest of her life.

And unless I kept Stan talking long enough that someone would come rescue me, or I could figure out a way to rescue myself, so would I.

I turned to him, and tried to focus on keeping my eyes away from the bed and my voice even. "Is this Enrique's place?"

Stan shook his head, looking around with a sneer. "The faggot's."

"Juan lives here?" It was the last place I would have guessed he'd live, but taking another look around, I could see why he'd like it. The boat might be old and a bit decrepit, and the furniture not exactly new, but it was put together with care and a certain amount of style. Colorful throw pillows on the couch and bed, a bright comforter. And Juan had always had a sort of obsession with Captain Tony Tarracino; he'd told me once that the only thing he wanted to do as a kid, was grow up to work at Captain Tony's Bar. I guess living on a houseboat was just another part of the dream.

"I'm curious," I said, both because I was and because I'd

decided to try to keep him talking for long enough that I might avoid getting raped. "Ty had a theory—"

Stan's face went stony at the sound of the name, and I backpedaled.

"What happened to Juan... was that really just so that Detective Fuentes would be distracted and wouldn't be at the Courthouse on the day you planned to escape?"

Stan smirked. "Am I good, or am I good?"

Not all that good, if we'd figured it out. Although he'd gotten away with it so far, so maybe I shouldn't say anything.

"So that was really the only reason why? You asked your buddy to beat up Juan just so you'd have a better chance of getting away?"

"I asked him to kill him," Stan said. "What's one less faggot? But he couldn't even do that right. Fucking moron."

Or maybe, hopefully, Stan's accomplice had decided that he didn't want to be an accessory to murder. That assault was as far as he'd go. Still too far, if you asked me, but better than it could have been.

"What's this thing you've got about the Fuentes family, anyway? Carmen wouldn't go out with you in high school, so you raped her, and had her brother beat up, and kidnapped her, and raped her again, and knocked her brother out so you could steal his car keys... That's assault on a police officer, by the way. You keep adding to your charges. Not to mention what you did when you shot Martoni and Sullivan. When they catch you again, they'll put you in jail and throw away the key."

"They have to catch me first," Stan said, with a smirk that said clearly that he had no fear of that happening.

I scowled at him. "You're not all that, you know. We... Enrique and Ty found you this morning. They'll find you again."

The smirk disappeared. "Nobody'll come looking for me here. So don't get any ideas about anyone coming to rescue you."

"I don't see why not," I said. "I mean, it's logical that you'd be here. Sullivan's and Martoni's places were just sitting there empty because they were both in the hospital. Juan's also in the hospital. His place is also sitting empty. I bet you whatever you want that as soon as he gets a car, Ty will be on his way over here. Straight here."

"Then we'd best get started," Stan said and gestured with the gun. "On the bed."

Oops.

That hadn't been the plan. I had planned to keep him talking. But instead I'd only pushed him into acting faster.

"Wait a second. I still don't know whether it was Sullivan or Martoni who beat up Juan."

Stan grinned. "It'll give you something to think about."

Just lie back and think of Sullivan?

"No," I said.

Stan blinked. "What d'you mean, no?"

"I'm not getting on the bed."

"But I'll shoot you," Stan said. He lifted the gun, but in a sort of half-assed way, like he couldn't quite believe we were having this conversation.

I had a hard time believing it myself. I'd taken some self-defense classes right after coming back from Key West last year, and one thing the instructor had been adamant about, was that you don't argue with a man with a gun. Or a man with a knife. If you can get away from him without getting hurt, do it, but don't risk your life arguing with someone who has the ability to kill you.

Stan had the ability to kill me. I should probably just get on the bed and focus on surviving.

But damned if I could, or wanted to. My heart was beating like a voodoo drum, but I shook my head. If my voice wasn't entirely steady, I think that's understandable. "No, you won't. If you shoot me, I'll scream and bleed all over Juan's bedspread, and all over you, and you don't want that. Besides, people will hear the shot and come running."

It looked like he hesitated. I did have a point, after all. Not that I'd keep quiet if he tried to rape me, but there was no sense in bringing that up. He'd figure it out soon enough.

The gun was still pointed at me, but not in a very determined fashion. It was aimed at my knees more than my stomach or chest at the moment. If he shot me there, I might not be able to run away—and the sharks were likely to get me if I jumped in the water—but I'd survive.

I was so busy watching the gun and calculating what I would do if he shot me, that I wasn't watching Stan. When he backhanded me across the cheekbone and temple, it came out of the blue.

Oww!

Pain exploded in my head, and I staggered sideways. That brought me into contact with the sharp edge of the coffee table, and my legs buckled. Before I could fall all the way, Stan grabbed me and yanked me back up. He propelled me a couple feet across the floor and gave me a shove in the direction of the bed. "Next time," he informed me through clenched teeth, "do as I say."

I landed and bounced. Juan must like to jump on the bed.

I would have bounced all the way off on the other side if I could have. Instead, I fetched up against the wall with a thud. The boat rocked a little. It took me a second or two to scramble around from my knees to my butt, and by then Stan was on me. He was still holding the gun—I guess maybe it made him feel safer, or maybe he planned to use it to threaten me when we were in close quarters—but the proximity made me able to make a grab for it. My head was still pounding, and sick, oily waves of nausea rose in my throat. I certainly wasn't able to scream; if I opened my mouth, I'd probably throw up all over Stan. And while that wouldn't make him happy, and might even make him back off, it would also incapacitate me for the time that it took.

So I fought with my teeth gritted, my nails—which I keep short because I do a lot of typing—digging into the skin of Stan's wrist. I had both of my hands wrapped around the one with the gun, and for once, I wished I had nice, long, super-enforced talons—like Carmen's—that could really do some damage.

Stan, meanwhile, had a knee in my stomach and was trying to get his gun-hand free. I hung on like grim death. If he dropped the gun, it would probably hit me in the face and maybe even break my nose, but I didn't want him to be able to use it, so I fought on.

In the middle of everything, the gun went off with another almighty bang. The bullet shot up and hit the ceiling at an angle. And then it pinged off. No safe burial in leather and stuffing this time, and no small puff of dust. The boat was made of metal, so the only thing that happened was that a tiny flake of white paint dropped off the ceiling and fell. The bullet changed direction and kept going, straight toward the kitchen.

I think I screamed, but honestly, my ears were ringing so loudly from the rapport that I couldn't hear myself. I did hear the sound when the bullet hit the toaster and made it jump a foot in the air.

And from the doorway came a voice.

"I'd drop that gun if I were you, son."

The voice didn't belong to Ty. He wouldn't have had time to get here, anyway. No, my rescuer was the old guy with the bait bucket, whom we'd passed in the parking lot when we arrived. Except instead of a bucket of bait, now he was holding a sort of rifle with what looked like a sharp arrow poked into the end of it. Behind him, I could see several of the other boat owners we had passed on the way here peering over his shoulder.

Stan hesitated.

"This spear is three feet long, son," Bait Bucket told him. "It'll punch straight through you. And with a barb at the end, it'll hurt like hell coming out. You sure you want to risk it?"

Apparently Stan wasn't sure, because his hand went a bit limp.

"Go ahead, girl," Bait Bucket nodded to me. "Take it."

I took it. And turned it around and pointed it at Stan.

Best as I could figure out, there should still be a bullet left. Or maybe it was only the old six-shooters in Westerns that had six bullets; Stan's gun may have had more. But he'd used two on Sullivan and Martoni, and one in getting away from Martoni's house. Number four was buried in the backseat of Enrique Fuentes's car, and the one that had killed Juan's toaster was number five.

That was if he'd started with a full clip, of course. But there ought to be at least one bullet left, I figured. Enough to shoot him if he tried anything.

He didn't. He moved off me and then lifted his hands. The retirees from behind Bait Bucket swarmed through the door and down the stairs. They surrounded him and dragged him up and out into the sunshine. And with so many of them and only one of him, there wasn't a whole lot Stan could do. I imagine he might have considered making a break for it and jumping into the water, but between the Coast Guard patrolling the sea and Bait Bucket on shore with his spear gun, I figured he knew his chances were poor.

"You all right, young lady?" Bait Bucket asked and extended a hand to me. Not the one holding the weapon. The other one.

I took it and let him haul me up from the bed. "Yes, thank you. What happened?"

"Recognized him," Bait Bucket said. "His face has been on the news every day this week. I don't know what he thought he was doing, walking around outside in broad daylight. Everyone in the marina knew who he was. And everyone in the marina knows Juan Fuentes. And that ain't Juan."

I shook my head. No, it wasn't.

"You know Juan?" Bait Bucket asked.

"A little."

"You know how he's doing?"

I told Bait Bucket I'd been informed that they'd be bringing Juan out of the induced coma later today. "So I assume he's doing all right. Or will be doing all right, with a little more time."

Bait Bucket nodded. "If there's anything he needs, tell him to get in touch. He's one of us." He turned toward the stairs to the outside, and then took a step back. "After you."

"Don't mind if I do," I said, and climbed the couple of steps up to the sunshine. And if I held onto the railing a little extra hard—because my knees were a bit wobbly—it's nobody's business but mine.

Ty came screeching into the parking lot a couple of minutes later, just behind the squad car with flashing lights and sirens that was coming to take Stan away. Bait Bucket had not only pulled out his spear gun and organized the other boat owners into attack formation, he had called 911 first, so they could be on the road as quickly as possible. If I were forty years older and wasn't already crazy about Ty, I'd marry Bait Bucket. A man who can handle all that, plus rescue a damsel in distress, is a keeper.

"Cassie!"

I turned around when I heard the shout, and saw Ty leap off a little crotch rocket motorcycle and run toward me, skirting the uniformed cops converging on Stan to drag him off into the squad car.

I managed a smile, although my face was really starting to hurt. And must be starting to turn black and blue, too, because his eyes narrowed. "What happened?"

"Stan," I said.

"He hit you?"

"It was my own fault. I wouldn't get on the bed."

"It was not your fault," Ty said. "Nothing that happened was your fault. It was his fault. All of it."

He shot a look over his shoulder that should have dropped Stan dead in his tracks, but since he was already inside the police car, it was hard to tell exactly how he reacted. Knowing him, he probably smirked.

"Just take him back to jail," I said, turning away. "Convict him, and lock him up, and lose the key. Make sure he can't hurt anyone else ever again."

Ty nodded. "The trial will resume tomorrow. With a few extra charges. Another rape and attempted rape, escape, assault on three police officers, breaking and entering, deprivation of liberty..."

"Is Enrique OK? And Carmen?"

"They should be at the hospital by now," Ty said, with a glance at his watch. "If you don't mind riding on the bike, I can take you there. You can give your statement to Enrique when he's awake."

"I'd like to see them," I admitted. "And Juan. Are they still waking Juan this morning?"

"As far as I know." He put an arm around my shoulders and guided me toward the bike, only stopping to shake Bait Bucket's hand on the way past, and to tell him thanks for saving the day. "The police will be by later to take your statement. And everyone else's. They're a little short-staffed right now, with three people laid up in the hospital."

Bait Bucket nodded. "I'll be here. We all will. You two take care, now."

We continued on toward the bike. The squad car with Stan in it drove past us, slowly, making for the entrance to the parking lot. I looked at it, but couldn't make out Stan's face through the window.

"He'll make it to where he's going this time, right?"

"With nobody to help him," Ty said, "yes."

"He never told me whether it was Sullivan or Martoni who helped him with the handcuffs. I asked, but he told me it would be something for me to think about while he..."

Ty's arm tightened around my shoulders, but his voice stayed even. "We'll figure it out. Once Juan's awake, he'll be able to tell us."

All the more reason to get to the hospital. I quickened my steps, and next to me, Ty did the same.

CHAPTER
Thirteen

By the time we reached the Lower Keys Medical Center, Enrique Fuentes had been examined and patched up and declared good to go. Technically speaking, he had a negligible little concussion—his words—but with Stan to process back into jail and a lot more charges to file, and a trial to get back on track, not to mention the last few loose threads to wind up, he couldn't afford any downtime. So he'd promised the doctor he'd take it easy and would lie down if he started seeing double, and we found him sitting beside Juan's bed. Where Juan still had bandages wound around his head, Enrique had gotten away with losing a patch of hair on the side of his head to accommodate a large Band Aid.

Juan was still asleep, or maybe unconscious, but the various tubes and needles had been removed from his arms, leaving purple and yellow bruising behind.

"How long has it been?" Ty wanted to know, his voice soft, even though the whole point was to wake Juan so we could see how he was doing.

Enrique answered in the same hushed tones. "They stopped the medication at eight this morning. But it can take hours for it to work its way out of his body so he wakes up."

"What about Carmen?"

Enrique's face darkened. "She isn't here. They took her to Doctor Johnson at the women's clinic."

The same one where I'd been last year. Where they had treated all of Stan's victims. "Good choice," I said.

Enrique nodded, looking exhausted. "My mom's gone there to be with her. My dad's on his way home from work. He'll be here for Juan."

"And you?"

"I have to get back to work," Enrique said. "I was just sitting here for a while, hoping that he'll wake up so I can arrest Sullivan or Martoni before I leave. I don't have time to come back later."

Ty hid a smile. "I'd be happy to arrest Sullivan or Martoni for you," he said.

"Thanks, but he's my brother. I want to do the honors."

Hard to blame him for that.

He added, "Cassie looks a little worse for wear. Have you had that looked at?" He glanced at my face.

I lifted a hand to it, self-consciously, and winced when it hurt. "I haven't even looked at it myself. Maybe I should."

"Mirror in there," Enrique said and nodded to the bathroom door. And then realized he probably shouldn't have, because he turned a shade paler.

"I'll go grab some ice," Ty said, heading for the hallway. "I'll be right back."

He went outside at the same time as I ducked into the tiny, adjacent bathroom and turned on the light.

Oh, boy. Yeah, I did look like I'd taken a beating. Funny; it had hurt at the time, but not enough that I had thought it would turn into this.

One whole side of my face was bruised and swollen, from temple almost to chin. And because Stan had caught the edge of my eye socket, my eye was turning black. I looked like I'd gone a couple of rounds in a boxing ring. And when I pressed on it, it hurt.

"Here." Ty showed up in the doorway with a cold compress he must have charmed out of one of the nurses. "Hold this against it for a few minutes. It's probably too late, but it might make you feel better."

"Maybe." If the skin was already turning purple and blue-black, there wasn't much that could be done, I figured. Nonetheless, I held the compress to my cheek, wincing, as I went back to sit down by the bed. Only to see Enrique leaning forward, intently.

"His eyelids fluttered."

Ty and I leaned closer, too. He was right; Juan's eyelids did flutter.

"Juan?" Enrique said. His voice came out froggy, and he had to clear his throat and try again. "'mano? You in there, bro?"

We all watched, holding our collective breath, as Juan's eyes opened. He blinked at the ceiling, disoriented, for a few moments before his attention moved to Enrique. This tongue flicked out to moisten his lips and he managed a whisper. "Hospital?"

Enrique nodded.

"Why?"

"You were mugged," Enrique said, going with the simplest and quickest explanation.

Juan's gaze tracked to me, and the bruises on my face. "My fault?"

"No," Enrique said, at the same time as I shook my head.

"Not your fault. Do you remember walking me home from Captain Crow's Monday night?"

Juan nodded. It was a tiny nod, just the barest movement of his head. If I felt rough, I could only imagine how he must feel. "We got mugged?"

"*We* didn't. You walked me to the motel and then you went

off on your own. You had a... you were meeting someone, you said."

Juan blinked.

"Do you remember?" Enrique prompted.

"I went to Bobby's." Juan moistened his lips again. "Met a guy. Had a few drinks. Was going home when..." He shook his head.

"Do you remember being at the cemetery?"

"No..." Juan said, his eyes drifting shut again.

"The guy you were meeting..."

Juan didn't answer, and for a second I thought he'd fallen back asleep. Enrique must be more used to his brother's reactions, because he leaned over the bed. "Listen." And then he switched into Spanish, much too fast for me to follow. All I could catch was a word here and there, but it was enough— along with the numerous mentions of Stan's name, which is the same in any language—to know that Enrique was telling Juan everything that had happened over the past two days.

As Enrique talked, the expression on Juan's face went from defiant to disbelieving to shocked. When Enrique started slowing down, probably because he was nearing the end of the story, Juan's gaze tracked to me and the ice I was still holding to my cheek. "You OK?" he whispered.

I nodded. "The old guy with the spear gun saved the day. You have great neighbors."

He smiled faintly. "My boat OK?"

"You have a bullet mark on your ceiling. And you'll need a new toaster. Other than that, it's fine. Same as it was."

"Stan's back in jail," Enrique said. "We're going back to court tomorrow. I'll be adding a lot of new charges to the ones we already had. And I'd like to nail down his accomplice before I leave here today. But he wouldn't tell Cassie who helped him with the handcuffs."

Juan didn't speak.

"We know it was either Dave Sullivan or Cody Martoni," Enrique added. "He beat you up, 'mano. And he helped Stan escape. That's not the kind of cop I want in my department."

We waited for Juan to decide to talk. After a few seconds, Ty added, "What he did goes way beyond trying to keep someone's sexual preferences quiet so he won't get in trouble, Juan. Because of what he did, you're here, and another cop—an innocent cop—got shot. Your brother got a concussion, Cassie could have died, and Carmen—"

"Cody," Juan said. He closed his eyes. "The guy I was meeting Monday night was Cody Martoni."

I glanced at Ty. He glanced back. And then we both looked at Enrique, who looked like Juan had punched him in the gut.

Maybe he'd have been happier if Juan had fingered Dave Sullivan.

Or maybe not. Maybe he'd have gotten that sick look on his face no matter which name Juan had said. Either way, Enrique lost—and had to arrest—another cop he'd trusted up until now.

"Get some sleep," he told Juan and got to his feet, more heavily than usual. "Dad's on his way. I'll stop in later."

I don't know whether Juan heard him or not. He might already have been asleep. Or he might have been pretending to be asleep, so he wouldn't have to watch Enrique head out the door to arrest someone I thought Juan had maybe hoped he could care about.

It wasn't a long walk. Martoni was still just around the corner. It took half a minute to get there, even with Enrique dragging his feet.

Martoni was looking a little better today. Still hooked up to all his wires and tubes, but with a little more color in his cheeks. When we walked in, he managed a smile. Until Enrique told him, his voice heavy, "Cody Martoni, you're under arrest for assault and dereliction of duty and facilitating an escape from custody—"

Then Martoni's eyes bulged and his mouth dropped open. He shook his head violently, so violently that he turned pale.

"Juan's awake," Ty told him. "He said you and he got

together on Monday night. At Bobby's Monkey Bar."

Martoni managed a whisper. "That's not illegal."

"No," Ty agreed. "But assault is."

Martoni shook his head. "I didn't touch him, man. I wasn't anywhere near when that happened. I know I should have walked him home. But he didn't... we weren't..." He flushed.

They weren't on those terms yet, and Juan hadn't invited him to walk him home. Or so I assumed. It fit with what Juan had told me on Monday night. Not a date. But drinks with someone he'd liked enough to dress up for. The beginning of something.

"Try again," Enrique said. "Because I don't buy that some stranger turned up out of the blue to mug my brother the day before you helped Stan Laszlo escape from custody."

"Not just mug him," I shot in. "Stan said he told you to kill Juan. But that you messed up."

Both Ty and Enrique stared at me, wide-eyed. So did Martoni.

"You're crazy," he said hoarsely. "I wouldn't hurt Juan. I like him. I was hoping..." He trailed of.

"So who did?" Enrique wanted to know.

Martoni shook his head. "I dunno, man. I wasn't there. Last time I saw him, he was walking away from Bobby's. I should have gone with him, but he didn't ask. I thought maybe he didn't want..."

Enrique and Ty exchanged a glance. I was inclined to believe Martoni, and it looked like maybe they were, too. He certainly sounded sincere.

"What happened at lunch yesterday?"

Martoni took a breath. "Stan was moaning in the back seat. Sully stopped the car. I opened the back door to see what was wrong. And he shot me."

"Did you open the cuffs?"

Martoni shook his head. Firmly. A bit more firmly than I figured he ought to, since he turned pale. But his voice was as strong as he could make it. "No, sir, Detective. I did not."

Enrique nodded. "Get some rest. Your folks are on their way."

Martoni nodded, too, and sank back against the pillows, looking exhausted. We were halfway out the door when he spoke again. "Stan?"

Enrique looked at him over his shoulder. "He's back in custody."

We all watched Martoni's face, looking for a flicker of fear, of worry. But there was nothing. Just a smile.

"Sullivan," Ty said when we were outside in the hallway.

Enrique nodded. He turned to me. "Were you telling the truth about what Stan said?"

"That he asked his accomplice to kill Juan? Yes. At least that's what he told me." Whether he was telling the truth was another matter entirely, but he had no reason to lie.

"I'm gonna kill him," Enrique said, jaw tight as he set off down the hallway. Ty and I exchanged a glance and hurried after.

We found Sullivan sitting up in a chair, dressed in a pair of loose sweatpants and a Key West PD T-shirt. He looked like he was on his way out, and maybe he was. Maybe we'd caught him just in time.

Enrique didn't pull any punches, or waste any words. "We've got Stan," he told Sullivan.

And then we all watched Sullivan turn pale.

Enrique sighed. "David Sullivan, you're under arrest for assault, and dereliction of duty, and facilitating an escape from custody—"

He reached for his handcuffs, and stumbled back when Sullivan came out of the chair and gave him a shove. Sullivan headed for the door at a stumbling run that, I'm sure, must have hurt his wounded leg.

I scrambled out of the way, and watched as Ty took him down, quickly and efficiently. "Cuffs," he said, holding out a hand, his knee in the middle of Sullivan's back. I took them from Enrique, who was still trying to get to his feet, and handed them over. Ty snapped them over Sullivan's wrists, and yanked him up.

"It was Stan!" Sullivan said, rattling the restraints. "He made me do it."

"Knock it off." Ty shook him.

"He wanted me to kill Juan," Sullivan babbled. "I didn't. That's gotta weigh, right? Right? That I coulda killed him and didn't?"

"Juan isn't the only person who got hurt," Enrique told him, on his feet now. "You let Stan go, and Stan attacked Cassie."

Sullivan looked at me, and then quickly away before he could meet my eyes. Ty's jaw tightened, but he didn't speak.

"He attacked Carmen, too," Enrique continued. "And shot at Agent Connor. That could easily have gone wrong. And you're lucky I just have a concussion."

Not surprisingly, Sullivan had no answer to that one, either.

"And he shot Martoni in the gut and almost killed him. All because you opened his handcuffs."

There was a moment of silence. I guess we were all waiting for Sullivan to respond, to say something, anything. But he didn't.

"What were you afraid he was going to do to you?" Enrique wanted to know, his voice calmer now that he'd laid out his case. "What did he have on you, that would make you agree to help him?"

Sullivan laughed, a little bitterly, I thought. "I've known him since we were kids, man. We grew up together. When I came back from Iraq, he's the one who got me the job with the PD. When he asked if I'd share some of the drugs the VA gave me for depression and to help me sleep, wasn't like I could say no."

I gaped at him. "You're the one who gave him the drugs. The drugs he used on the girls. And on me."

"I didn't know what he was gonna use 'em for," Sullivan

said. "Not at first. It's a couple years ago. I thought he just wanted to relax. It ain't easy, being a cop."

Nobody responded to that. "When did you figure out what he was doing?" Ty wanted to know.

"Not till last year."

"So last Spring Break, you knew Stan was using the drugs you gave him to rape girls. And you didn't say anything?"

"I talked to him," Sullivan said. "And he said if I said anything, he'd take me down with him. Say I'd known all along what he was doing. That I was doing it, too."

"And did you?"

"No!" Sullivan shook his head. "God, no. I saw enough of that shit in Iraq."

No doubt. Although that wasn't an excuse for what he'd done, and what he'd allowed to happen. Even so, I did feel a little bad for him. But just a little.

"Stay here." Ty held me back as Enrique started marching Sullivan down the hallway toward the elevator. "They don't need us for this."

I glanced at him. "Are you sure? Sullivan might try to get away once they get outside."

"He's cuffed," Ty said. "And after what he did to Juan, Enrique won't take any chances. He'll put a bullet in him before he lets him get away."

Alrighty, then. "So it's over."

"It ain't over till the fat lady sings. Or something like that."

"Mackenzie isn't fat."

Ty's face cracked in a smile. "I wasn't talking about Mackenzie. It'll be over when the trial is finished and Stan has been sentenced to a hundred years in prison. Or whatever the maximum penalty is for what he did. When he's locked up, and can't get out, and all we have to do is watch him rot, that's when it'll be over."

"Next week?"

"Could be next week," Ty said and pushed the button for the elevator.

"Can you stick around?"

"As long as it takes," Ty said, and pulled me through the sliding doors.

Epilogue

"I wish Paula could have seen this," I told Ty.

It was a week later, and we were sitting at a table in Captain Crow's Bar, watching not just Austin, but Mackenzie, too, up on the little stage at the back of the room, entertaining the crowd of Spring Breakers. Most of them probably had no idea that America's Country Sweetheart herself, along with her significant other, were providing tonight's entertainment. Most of them were drunk out of their minds, and likely wouldn't recognize their own mothers if they were to show up. But at least one guy had his phone out and was filming the performance. By tomorrow morning, it would have gone viral.

"Did you call her?"

I nodded. I had, the evening the verdict came down in Stan's trial. Guilty on all counts, including the new ones—not that there was any doubt. He was sentenced to enough years in prison that both Paula and I would be grandmothers by the time he saw daylight again. "She just couldn't come back. It's expensive, flying back and forth from Wisconsin to Key West."

"Maybe you should ask Mackenzie to dedicate a song to her. That way, when the guy with the phone uploads his video to YouTube tomorrow, Paula can hear it."

"That's a good idea."

I gave him a beaming smile before I twitched out of the arm he had put around my shoulders and made my way to the back of the room. On the way, I passed Quinn and James, who were twined around each other at a table. They were so busy they didn't even notice me walking by. Good thing the artist James Hunt wasn't as famous as Mackenzie and Austin yet, or the tabloids would have gotten an eyeful.

Up by the stage I waited for a break in the music, and then waved Mackenzie over. "Can you sing a song for me?"

She grinned. "Sure, girlfriend."

"Actually, it's not for me. It's for Paula. She was here last year. One of the girls Stan raped. And she was here last week, too, to testify. She really wanted to meet you. And I told her she could, but when Stan escaped she went home. So I thought maybe you could sing a song for her. And she could watch it on YouTube and hear that it was dedicated to her."

"Of course," Mackenzie said. "What song do you want?"

"The one about things getting better? Being strong and hanging on and waiting for things to get better?"

"You got it," Mackenzie said. "We'll do it after this one. I'll tell Austin." She ambled off across the little stage, the heels of her boots banging against the worn wood of the floor, and her skirt swaying around her thighs.

I turned and headed back to Ty, although I stopped beside Quinn on my way past and leaned down. "Get a room."

She didn't shriek and jump, as I had halfway hoped. Instead, she just turned to me. "We have a room. With a view and a king size bed and everything."

"Way to rub it in," I said. "Ty and I are sharing a postage stamp."

"That's what happens when you get involved with the law," James told me, in that snooty, upscale accent of his.

Quinn wrinkled her brows. "You can come stay at the Cove Suites, you know. I'm sure they'd find a room for you."

I wasn't. Not in the middle of Spring Break. "That's OK. We're happy where we are."

"You sure?" Quinn said.

"I'm positive. Carry on."

I walked away, while they went back to what they'd been doing. They might as well just go home, because there was no way they had any idea what was going on around them.

I was just sitting down next to Ty when Mackenzie began the windup for the song I had asked for. "This one goes out to Cassie," she said; I arched my brows, "and to her friend Paula in Wisconsin, who couldn't be here with us tonight. It's gonna be all right, baby. Just stay strong and hold on and wait for things to get better."

As she began singing, and as the crowd was swaying back and forth—just as much due to being shitfaced drunk as to the music—Ty reached over and took my hand. "Cassie."

I smiled at him. "Ty. Thanks for staying."

The trial had been concluded a couple of days ago. He should probably have gone back to Quantico or wherever he reported in between assignments. But instead he'd decided to spend the rest of the week with me, in that cramped little room at Richardson's Motel. Just the two of us, a miniscule shower, and a bed.

We'd spent a lot of time in that bed, and not just because there was nowhere else to sit.

"I had some time saved up," Ty said. "Cassie—"

"Well, I appreciate it. I'm sure there's another assignment lined up you have to take. They probably have something in mind already. Did you postpone a job for me?"

He shrugged, which I took to mean yes. If he hadn't, he probably would have said so.

"Where are you going next?"

"Chicago," Ty said.

I blinked. "You've already been to Chicago."

"And now I'm going back."

"But... I thought you left Chicago. You know, after...?"

He shook his head. "I never left. I just stayed away from you. I figured you needed time."

I guess I had needed time. Time to realize that being without him wasn't any easier than being with him. More distance didn't make the worry any easier to take. And it would take a lot more than not officially being his girlfriend anymore to make me stop caring about what happened to him.

"I won't be doing undercover work forever," he told me, while Mackenzie sang about staying strong and holding on and waiting for things to get better. "In a couple years, I'll be too old. I'll join the profilers and spend my time sitting at a desk. The most dangerous thing I'll be doing, is interviewing a serial killer while he's safely behind bars."

"Like in *Silence of the Lambs*?" Because that sounded dangerous to me.

"Nothing like in *Silence of the Lambs*," Ty said firmly. "Very boring."

If he said so.

He shook his head. "I know it's a lot to ask, Cassie. I can't offer you anything. I mean, I could, but..."

"Anything?"

"Marriage," Ty said. "I can't offer to marry you. I mean, I guess I could, but..."

I looked at him—he guessed he could?—and he blew out a breath and ran a hand through his hair. "It's too soon, Cassie. We don't know each other very well. We need more time together first. And you haven't even finished college yet. You have no idea what's out there. It's a big world. And..."

"I agree," I said, before he could continue to list all the other reasons why he couldn't propose and I couldn't say yes. "You're right. It's too soon." I wasn't ready for that level of commitment. "I want to keep seeing you. But I'm not ready to get married."

"If you can just hold on a couple of years," Ty said, "things will get better. I promise."

"I believe you." When he looked at me like that, I'd believe anything he said.

"Being involved with law enforcement is hard. And I understand if you don't want to deal with it, but I thought maybe you'd give me another chance. Give us another chance. And see where we end up."

"I think I might be able do that," I said, and leaned in to kiss him.

ABOUT THE

Sign up for Jenna's email newsletter and be the first to learn about new releases, sales, exclusive newsletter reads, and other exciting things.

New York Times and *USA Today* bestselling author Jenna Bennett (Jennie Bentley) writes the Do It Yourself home renovation mysteries for Berkley Prime Crime and the Savannah Martin real estate mysteries for her own gratification. She also writes a variety of romance for a change of pace. Originally from Norway, she has spent more than twenty five years in the US, and still hasn't been able to kick her native accent.

For more information, please visit Jenna's website:
www.JennaBennett.com

CHASING ME
Jennifer Probst

It was supposed to be a love story...

I knew she was out of my league but I didn't care. Looking back, I wonder if I hadn't pursued her, would things have turned out differently? Is it Fate that determines our choices in life? God? Free will? Or just plain old innate selfishness?

I got her, of course. There hadn't been a girl I wasn't able to seduce. Problem was she seduced me right back, body, mind, and soul. She possessed me, tormented me, and showed me a world that was so bright and pure I was almost blinded.

Didn't she know after such a drug I could never settle for less? Didn't she realize no matter how many times I screwed up, or broke her heart, or bent her to my will, I'd never be able to let her go?

If I hadn't known such intensity existed, would it have been better for both of us?

True love, the real kind, isn't nice and sweet and pure. No, it's dirty, and sinful, and messy. It's like ripping a chunk of flesh from your body and watching yourself bleed out in slow, helpless intervals until you thankfully pass out.

This isn't a love story. But it's the only story I got.

LOSING US
Jen McLaughlin

When it all comes crashing down...

Everything I thought I had with Austin Murphy--safety, stability, the normalcy I crave but my celebrity lifestyle rarely allows--was ripped away in one night. I wanted to surprise him, but the joke was on me. Now I don't know if I ever really knew him at all.

Someone has to pick up the pieces...

Mackenzie Forbes was everything I ever wanted and the one person I didn't deserve. When a past mistake costs me the girl I love, I'll do everything I can to get her back. We both have demanding careers and family secrets darkening our pasts, but I need Mackenzie in my future.

Sometimes everything you have to give just isn't enough...

Made in the USA
Middletown, DE
25 September 2023

39253614R00090